FATED TO THE ALIEN HEALER

WARRIORS OF TAVIKH
BOOK FIVE

ERIN HALE

Fated to the Alien Healer
© 2024 by Erin Hale
Cover design by Natasha Snow

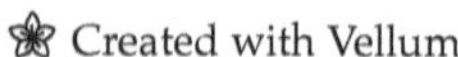 Created with Vellum

CONTENT WARNINGS
*MAY CONTAIN SPOILERS

As someone who doesn't have any triggers, it is often hard for me to know what might be a trigger for others. I have done my best to include what I think could potentially be triggering for someone. If I have not included yours, I apologize and hope you reach out so I know for the future.

Discussion of SA
Discussion of suicide
Violence
Anxiety / panic attacks
Nightmares about blood and death

CHAPTER 1

*If your book opens to this page, please refer to prior page for CW

NINE MONTHS AGO

Zara

I really fucked up this time. Not even a little bit either. It's not going to matter that it wasn't my fault. Like always, according to Clifton and Priscilla Black, I'll be the one to blame. I ruined my mother's figure. My father's friends and business associates pity him because he didn't have boys to take over his business. Those are the least of my sins.

I'm messy and chaotic and I don't fit into the box they tried to shove me in and haven't for a long time. I'm essentially a burden. A mistake they never wanted in the first place. At least when I was little, I got to share the misery with Amelia. But she's been gone for more than half my life, so I get to bear the full weight of the elder Blacks' disappointment and apathy.

Just thinking about my sister brings tears to my eyes. There are days when I wish I could hate her for leaving me. For *abandoning* me. But I can't. Not knowing what I know. Instead, I wish I had been old enough to understand what it was she'd been going through. That she could have talked to me like I talked to her even if my problems were juvenile in comparison. She'd been more than my sister. She'd been my confidante. My best friend in the whole world. Practically my mother, in fact. It didn't matter that she was only nine years older. She made everything better. She made me feel loved. Then…she was gone. And to our parents, it's like she never existed.

I get up from my bed and pace my bedroom. The pristine —everything in its place because that's how Priscilla requires it—bedroom. Although these days, it feels more like a cage. Maybe I wouldn't be so on edge if there was shouting down below. God forbid Clifton or Priscilla Black raise their voice though. Then again, they don't need to. Not when every sneer, every disdainful stare, every disappointed sigh says it all. I chew at a nail already chewed raw. It started after Amelia was gone. What began as a nervous—yet soothing—habit became my first small act of rebellion. It may seem ridiculously minor, but chewed-up, ragged nails don't fit the Black image.

Perfection has to be maintained at all times.

A bitter snort erupts out of my nose. What a joke. Perfection is merely an illusion my parents hide behind. They have no idea I see through it and have for a long time. It gives me the tiniest bit of sadistic pleasure to fuck with them on occasion. At least it did until now. Because, after this, the shame is real. And ugly. It's like a cancer weaving an insidious path through me. I suck in a ragged breath, trying not to break down. I've had years of practice hiding my emotions. I'm not going to cave now. *Especially* not now.

Muted footsteps grow louder until they come to a stop in front of my door and there's a single knock before it opens without me giving permission for the person to enter.

"Your father will see you in his office now, Miss Black," my *keeper*, Sylvia, announces in her usual condescending tone like I'm some visitor who had an appointment.

Without a thank you, I shoulder past her, and with my head held high and my back ramrod straight, I march to the room I hate the most. It feels more like a mausoleum, filled with so many ghosts, including the person I used to be. Knowing I won't disobey, Sylvia doesn't follow to make sure I don't dawdle. I reach Clifton's office—I stopped thinking of him as dad a long time ago—take in a deep, bracing breath and push the cracked door farther open.

Seated behind the god-awful glass and metal monstrosity he calls a desk, with his hands resting on its surface and his fingers intertwined, is my father. His light brown hair is swept back off his broad forehead and there's a hint of gray at his temples. Hardly any lines mar his face. How could they? He never smiles.

Off to the side, perfectly perched on a brown leather wing-back chair, with her hands folded in her lap is the woman who gave birth to me. Her blonde hair, so similar to mine, is carefully coiffed without a single strand out of place. None would dare. Similar to her husband, she has nary a wrinkle. Clifton glares while Priscilla glances away dismissively.

"For the last year I have either ignored or put up with your nonsense and utter disregard for the Black name. You have cost me thousands of credits cleaning up your messes and making them go away. Our family has a reputation to uphold. One that dates back hundreds of years. Yet, in the span of twelve months you have managed to tarnish that sterling reputation. And for what? You have gained nothing from your little rebellions other than to become a laughingstock amongst the upper tier."

I grit my teeth to hold back the curse threatening to escape, because fuck those people.

"What is worse is you have made your mother and me laughingstocks," Clifton continues. "This little escapade of yours is not something that can be swept under the rug. Do you know how many people have seen that disgusting video? Already, the Board has been bombarding my comm with calls for my resignation. You have embarrassed your mother. More important, you have embarrassed me. It's bad enough that you've made a mockery of yourself this past year, but now I am being dragged into your stupid decisions."

My cheeks heat and that familiar shame spirals through me. Still, I keep my mouth shut. Which is, apparently, the wrong thing to do. Clifton slams his palms on his desk, and I flinch. So does my mother.

"Don't you have anything to say?" he raises his voice.

I have a lot to say, actually, but none of it you'll like. "I'm sorry."

"That's it? You're sorry?" Disdain drips from his tone.

Despite my attempt to keep my emotions in check, my eyes burn with unshed tears and I sniffle. I blink them away, though, refusing to shed them in front of these people who don't care about my feelings.

"Yes. I'm sorry." That's all Clifton is getting out of me. If he or Priscilla showed an ounce of compassion for what happened to me, maybe I'd give them more.

My father sneers and laces his fingers together again. Only now, he leans back in his chair and lays them across his waist. "You've left me no choice, Zara. This is no one's fault but your own."

I blink in confusion. No choice for what?

"You will return to your room. Sylvia has packed a bag for you. I don't care where you go, but you are no longer welcome in this home. You have caused enough harm to the Black name. I will not let you destroy it any more than you already have," Clifton announces with a note of finality. "Do not come back. If you try to use my influence to help yourself in any way, it will not be given. As of today, you have ceased being a member of this family. I am done letting you ruin your mother and me. You are dismissed."

I stand there for several seconds. "I don't understand."

"What is there to not understand? You will take the few belongings I am allowing you to have, and you're leaving this house. We are finished with you, Zara. You have disgraced this family for the last time."

"You're kicking me out." I don't even phrase it as a question. It's nothing but a breathed statement of disbelief. Instead of the person responsible, I'm the one who continues to suffer. Against my will, tears well in my eyes, and a single drop spills over to race down my cheek. I hate myself for shedding it.

My gaze darts between the two people who are supposed to love me unconditionally. My father raises a brow expectantly while my mother sniffs with a hint of disdain, even though she won't meet my eyes. She continues to stare somewhere on the other side of the room. Certainly not at me. I lock gazes with my father.

"Why do you hate me?"

Clifton brushes a nonexistent piece of lint off his suit jacket front. "I don't hate you."

"You don't love me though, either, do you?" When he doesn't answer, I take in a ragged breath through my nose and nod. "I see."

Another minute passes. Or maybe seconds, but it's clear all that's going to be said has been. I turn my back on the people who turned theirs on me long before today and head for the door. For only a heartbeat, I hesitate at the threshold. Whether it's because I'm waiting for one of them to call me back—to tell me they're sorry and they didn't mean it—or because I should say something flippant or for some other reason entirely, I'm not sure. But none of those things happen. Instead, I follow the same path I'd taken to get here back to my room.

Sure enough, Sylvia waits inside. A single suitcase lies on top of the bed. I walk across the room, grab the handle, and drag it off the bed. At least she was kind enough to pack it full, although who knows what's inside. Maybe nothing I can actually use. I won't ask though. I won't give her the satisfaction. Once again, I head for a door and hesitate at its threshold. Only this time, I glance over my shoulder.

"I'm the one who told Grayson you were fucking Charles behind his back and I'm not even a little bit sorry." So much self-satisfaction courses through me at her wide-eyed expression and gaping mouth. "He deserved better than you and now he's found her. I hope the fact that Grayson's happier now than he ever was with you eats away at your shitty, hate-filled heart."

In a petulant gesture, I give her my biggest smile and my middle finger. Then I head out into the hallway, into the elevator, and then into the atrium of our building. Motorized bots carry various items in their outstretched arms as they enter and exit the service elevators. It's one of the reasons we moved in here. We had our own personal delivery system. Of course, they were all built by the company on whose Board Clifton sits. I dodge a couple of them all while wondering why my vision is so blurry.

It isn't until I step outside onto the busy pedestrian platform that I realize I'm blinded by tears. At least no one's paying me any attention. All the people walking past are focused on themselves. Not a single one of them notices me standing there with a suitcase in my hand and nowhere to go. I have more acquaintances than I can count, but all the friends I have were shared with Bryce. There's no way in hell I'm going to comm any of them.

I track my surroundings until I'm snagged by the bright lights of a massive electronic marquee. Different advertisements appear on it, pause long enough for a bystander to read its message, then dissolve, only to be replaced by the next one. A large yellow, purple, and black planet materializes on the screen. Across it float the words "Want to experience a brand-new world? One with plenty of land, where you can live peacefully and quietly and away from all the chaos of the city? Why not head to Tavikh?"

More info slides across the massive screen, but I don't pay much attention. My brain keeps playing the first part over and over. A brand-new world. Peace. Quiet. No chaos. All the things Amelia and I used to whisper about in the dark. How wonderful it would be to get away from everything. Away from Clifton and Priscilla. Just the two of us. We'd have a cute little house like they had a couple hundred years ago with stucco exterior and flowerbeds under the front windows.

It had been a completely unrealistic fantasy, but I'd held onto it all these years. As the image of the planet dissolves and another one replaces it—the face of a woman wanted for questioning regarding the murder of a CEO of some tech company— I remain standing there.

A warm feeling fills me. It reminds me of how I felt whenever Amelia hugged me. She'd been soft and squishy and gave the best hugs. They were the only ones I'd ever received in my entire life.

I've gone more than seventeen years without her arms around me. Except this feeling that's growing inside makes me think maybe she's telling me something. That this is my chance to do what we'd always dreamed about. To go. For her. Since she'll never be able to.

There's nothing for me here on Earth. I don't have any credits, and even if I somehow made my way down to the bottom tier—I shudder at the thought—I have no skills. Not a single one. It's as though I was purposefully left helpless. Reliant on the goodwill of Clifton and Priscilla Black.

Well, fuck that.

I'm getting on the next ship and I'm going to Tavikh to live my best life ever. Not only for myself, but for Amelia.

CHAPTER 2

Present Day

Kyler

While joy grows in my heart, so does sorrow, as I watch my apprentice and her mate exit the tent and head back to their own, Jodah's tail wrapped around Sage's waist. She latches onto his arm and leans in close as they walk side-by-side. My sorrow is not because I wish for her to be my mate. I am happy for her and Jodah. But their mating is a reminder that I have just passed forty cold seasons and still remain alone. I am beginning to resign myself to the fact I most likely always will be.

Instinctively, my gaze searches out bari-colored hair slightly different than my own even knowing its owner is not wandering around the village, but rather has hidden herself in her usual place working on her craft. I shake off the pointless task and return within the tent where I feel most at home.

Thanks to Sage, I have learned a new method of helping our people when they become ill and are unable to breathe while the cold dust falls. But now, it has melted away and signs of the warm season are visible. From the small buds of the flowering nenuphar bush to the blooming burim root that should be ready to be harvested within the next few turns of the sun. Either Sage or I will forage the forest and harvest the root when the time comes. It is something I find soothing so I may be the first to head out. Although being alone within the trees also gives me far too much time to think of things that will never be.

Soon, I have finished taking stock of the remaining inventory of healing remedies and make a mental note of what is low and needs to be replenished. I also need to increase the supply of kanet so I can grind it into its powder form in preparation of the Bohnari's arrival. While far more technologically advanced than us, our neighbors use one of our plants they say has special healing properties they cannot find on their home planet of Bohna. It is one more thing the end of cold season signals.

I have just straightened the last clay pot when an ear-splitting war cry comes from outside.

I race out of the tent and madness is before me. Smoke fills the sky and the crack of metal against metal echoes all around. My tribe brothers are locked in battle with Njeri warriors. Yelling females scatter and scoop up screaming kits to race away from the fighting. The shefira and her tribe sister, Maeve, spin in circles, their gazes searching as they call out for their other tribe sisters.

Tearing my gaze away from them, I sprint to the nearby weapon stores and rip back the hide flap that covers the entrance. I grab the nearest sword and rush out to help defend my people. A Njeri warrior locks eyes with me and charges. He swings with precision, and I block the strike sending a rattling vibration down my arms. My grip tightens so I do not lose my weapon, and I block a second strike that causes me to stumble. While I frequently spar with the other warriors to keep up my skills, I am a healer first and spend more time with my patients—as Sage calls them—and remedies.

The Njeri sneers with glee at my misstep, but I right myself, and this time it is I who goes on the offensive. All around us, females scream, but I cannot take my focus off my opponent or I will die a swift death. I land a minor blow that draws first blood, but the male across from me only laughs. My jaw tightens and I do not let him get to me. A flash of bari-colored hair appears nearby, and my gaze automatically goes in that direction. My heart leaps and settles that it is not the female whose presence never leaves my mind.

The distraction nearly costs me as a sharp stinging pain runs along my side. I can feel the blood cascading down, but I ignore it and the burning sensation that follows. Once again, I charge and get my own strike in, drawing blood a second time. In the distance, someone roars Zara's name. Somehow hearing it gives me strength, because I forge another path forward and discover a narrow opening. My sword finds its mark and I ram it into the abdomen of the Njeri. His eyes widen in shock and a pained moan spills from his mouth.

He stumbles this time, only I follow and use my tail to sweep his legs out from beneath him. With the momentum I have gained, I push the sword deeper as he falls to his back, and the tip of my blade runs through him until it exits the other side. Blood the color of the nenuphar flower spreads out beneath him to mar the bari-colored dirt he lies on. However, before I can celebrate, he takes a single desperate swing of his sword and manages to slice across the top of my leg. It gives out and I barely catch myself before I tumble on top of him.

With unmatched speed, I yank my weapon out of his body and stab him through the chest straight into his heart. The Njeri's body jerks and blood bubbles out of his mouth and slides down the side of his face. His eyes remain locked on mine until the life drains from them and they turn sightlessly toward the sky. Wetness coats my leg coverings, and I stumble backward.

Someone calls my name.

I jerk my head around and my gaze lands on Zander, our shefir. He too is covered in blood. Some of it his own, but most of it appears to be Njeri. Within his arms is a Tavikhi warrior who can barely stand on his own. I run to them, my steps unsteady from my own injury, and slide my shoulder beneath Rojtar's arm to help hold him up. Together, the shefir and I get our fallen tribe brother to the healer's tent.

To my relief, Sage, Remi, Eloise, and London—the shefira —are all inside as well. My apprentice is barking out orders as she works on one of the many injured warriors, and her three tribe sisters follow them. Zander and I place Rojtar onto a platform and I get to work on his injuries, which appear grievous. Benham storms inside with his mate, Maeve, at his side. Tears spill from her eyes and she rushes over to her tribe sisters.

"They took Zara," she cries and throws her arms around London.

I suck in a sharp breath and pause in my task. Rojtar moans and I curse my distraction and return to treating him. Except I cannot tune out the females' conversation.

"She was at the forge, but she's gone." Maeve's voice rises. "Benham found one of the most recent swords he crafted on the ground not far from the entrance. There was also blood. *Human* blood."

"Have all the tents that remain standing been checked?" Zander asks.

Benham steps forward. "Katem is searching still, but one of the elders is sure she saw a human with bari-colored hair being dragged by a Njeri warrior toward the hills."

"We're going to find her," Remi exclaims and turns to the shefir. "I'm going with the rescue party."

She says it as though there is no question one will take place. Considering she is a fierce warrior whose skill with both sword and staff rival some of the younger males, I am not surprised she is the first to volunteer. Her mate, Zydon, will be right at her side.

"I will go as well." The words spill from my lips before I realize I have said them.

Silence follows my statement. I glance up again from where I am suturing Rojtar's wounds closed to find everyone staring at me, but quickly return to my task. Zander, Zydon, and Remi discuss the rescue mission and argue about when to leave. Remi, of course, wants to go this instant, but we need to ready supplies and make sure we are prepared, especially as we will most likely be outnumbered.

By the time the two moons have risen fully in the sky, all three of our platforms are occupied and several beds of furs have been placed around the tent containing more wounded. The dead bodies—Tavikhi, human, and Njeri— have been gathered. Warriors have disposed of our enemies' and the tribespeople will prepare the life celebration for our fallen members, which number far more than any of us would like, including two mated tribespeople, which means that within the next turn of the sun, their mates will join them in the land of the goddess.

The village is somber. It will take many turns of the sun before dwellings have been repaired or rebuilt. The only people remaining within the healing tent, aside from the injured, are Sage and Jodah, who has remained present to make sure his mate takes care of herself as well as her patients.

With his help, the force that had previously been driving her to not sleep or eat for turns of the sun while treating both him and the Krijese kit brought here by his baba is not as strong. That does not mean she is any less dedicated to treating injured tribespeople, but her reasons for doing so have changed. No longer is she seeking forgiveness for something that occurred back on Earth.

I check on the last of the warriors before taking stock once again of the inventory that, since I last looked over it, has dwindled to almost nothing. Supplies were already on the low side due to the cold season. Sage approaches and comes to a stop on the nearest side of the table from where I stand.

Of all the humans, she is the one who has spent the most time here since she became my apprentice many lunar cycles before the shefira and her three tribe sisters arrived. Eloise's arrival had been unintentional. The ship she was traveling on had been attacked, and her escape pod crash landed on Tavikh. Deeka guided her to our planet where she was found by Zedam, the youngest brother of the shefir.

"I'm a little surprised you volunteered to go with the rescue team." Sage straightens an empty jar. Our supplies will need to be replenished as soon as possible.

She and I have become friends in the nine or more lunar cycles since she came to Tavikh, yet I am hesitant to explain my reasoning to her. It is a foolish hope that lives within me. Why would Deeka choose me as the mate for the beautiful female who I have watched from afar since the moment she arrived in the village? I have seen many seasons while there are a greater number of warriors younger than me who are also unmated.

All Zara has to do is touch one of the males. When she does, and his mating marks appear, I will once again be alone.

"We have been dealt a harsh blow, and with the amount of severely wounded warriors, Zydon and the rest of the males, as well as Remi, will need all the able-bodied help they can get. Despite how many Njeri did not survive today, their numbers are still greater than ours."

"Which is why I'm worried about you going," Sage says. "You're our healer, and we have seven injured—possibly dying—tribespeople. My skills aren't anywhere in comparison to yours. And as selfish as it may be, I'm worried I'm not going to be able to save them all if you leave."

I place a hand on her arm. "I am proud of the healer you have become. You have accomplished much while you have been here. However, no matter if it is you or I looking after them, every one of these warriors is now in Deeka's hands. If it is their time to join her, then there is nothing either of us can do. No Tavikhi fears traveling to the land of the goddess. It is where our ancestors await. Do not let the worry get to you. You will do the best you can to keep them here. But in the end, the goddess will decide their fate."

The humans do not hold the same beliefs as the Tavikhi so I understand it is often hard for them to comprehend our faith in Deeka. The goddess has never forsaken us. She will not do so now. Sage's gaze remains locked on mine for several beats before she finally gives a shallow nod and walks away to check on one of the injured.

When the rescue party sets out for the Njeri village, I will be with them.

CHAPTER 3

Zara

There isn't an inch of my body that doesn't hurt. I've lost track of how much time I've spent slung over this mammoth beast. The two moons have risen and set at least once. Of that much I'm aware. Or at least I think they have. It's kind of hard to judge how much time has passed. We've been traveling through the dense forest high up in the hills and very little light has managed to sift through the openings between the leaves and branches.

What I do know is during my conscious moments throughout this whole ordeal, I've been doing a lot of thinking. A dangerous pastime, my sister would have said. It's hard to believe six months ago I left Earth with dreams of a better place. A place with charming, idyllic cottages and a narrow, winding stream that bisected lush green lands where plants and flowers of all kinds grew. A maniacal laugh bubbles up my throat, but on its heels is the vomit that constantly churns from the upside-down ride.

Up until this dick head kidnapped me, life wasn't terrible. Certainly not what I'd envisioned on the two-month flight to Tavikh, but having five kick-ass friends and sexy eye-candy isn't such a bad gig. I mean, I've replaced the cottage with a hide tent I sleep in alone since my last roommate went and got herself hitched—mated. And the lush green lands are, in truth, fields of yellow grass—or bari as the Tavikhi call it—that resemble cotton balls on a skewer. The blue nenuphar flowers are pretty, at least. As are the red flowers of the trendafili bush, even if the prickly leaves hurt like hell when brushed against.

I picture the river running along one side of the village where we get all our water and where we bathe. At least, we'll be able to do so again now that the water is warming up and isn't colder than a witch's tit. Because I refuse to believe I've seen the last of the Tavikhi village. There's no way my friends—Remi especially—are going to just let these dip fuckers steal me away.

With all the blood settled inside my brain, I feel myself once again drifting out of consciousness. I don't fight the darkness this time. Within the dark is where Amelia resides. Realistically, I know she's dead and not holding conversations with me, but the part of me that misses her every single day embraces my madness. If having conversations with my dead sister helps me cope, then that's exactly what I'll do.

"I don't think we ever imagined one of us would get

kidnapped by some asshole when we dreamed of leaving Earth, did we?" I ask Amelia.

Her laughter, a sound I swore I'd never forget as long as I lived, rings out. "Of course it had to be you that got snatched, didn't it? You were never one to do the easy things in life, were you Zar?"

"Easy is for pussies." I snort and flinch against my pain.

During my rebellious stage, I liked to push Clifton and Priscilla's buttons. One of those buttons was my incessant need to be as vulgar as possible when I talked. They *hated* it when I swore. Which, of course, means my conversations were riddled with fucks and shits and various other creative swear words I came up with.

"You have to be careful," Amelia warns. "I know how much you want to fight back, but for my sake, please don't."

I rear away from her image. Of course I've fought back. Maybe it's earned me a few smacks across the face—okay, maybe more than a few—and having both my wrists and ankles bound. But man, kicking the bald Casper-the-ghost lookalike straight in the balls had been so worth it, just for his expression alone. I hope he can still taste them. "You want me to just roll over and let this asshole off easy? To do nothing while they take me away from my friends? My family? You want me to give up? Why? Because that's what you did?"

The second the hateful words are said, I want to call them back. Especially when she flinches. If she wasn't a complete figment of my addled and delusional mind, I'd even say she paled.

"Fuck, Lia, I'm sorry. That was a cunty thing to say."

Amelia shakes her head. "You always were stronger than me."

"That's not true." I reach for her hand, but considering this entire conversation is only in my head and she's not corporeal, mine goes through nothing but the ether.

"It is and we both know it." Her sorrow bleeds into me. "If I'd been stronger I wouldn't have left you alone to deal with Clifton and Priscilla. I would have stayed. For you. But I couldn't take the pain anymore."

"Of course you couldn't. Not after what Blaine did to you." Even knowing I can't touch her, I move my hand until it's lying beside hers. If I hold still long enough, I can imagine the heat from her fingertips. "I don't blame you, you know."

Amelia turns her gaze to me. "How did you find out?" she asks quietly.

"I overhead the bitch Sylvia talking about something she called 'the scandal'." My voice cracks. "After that I started snooping in Clifton's office and found the payments. Every year, on the anniversary of your death, the same number of credits was transferred into his account. It took me five months to track down Veronica and another three to wear her down before she told me."

My sister sighs. "Is she doing all right?"

Veronica had been Amelia's best friend. After Lia died, Veronica disappeared. One day she was there and the next…gone. Just like my sister. It was almost like neither of them had ever existed. I'd almost drained my allowance dry paying for information on her whereabouts. I'm honestly surprised I found her at all.

"Not really." I can still picture her dirt-marred cheeks and the sour-smelling, patched uniform she'd been wearing. It had been the hopelessness in her eyes I'll never forget, though. "Her family cast her out. Sent her to the bottom tier. The sanitation sector."

My sister sighs sadly. "That doesn't surprise me. Blaine belonged to a powerful family. There's no way they were going to let me, or anyone else, sully their precious son's name. I'm sure they paid a lot of credits to make Veronica go away. Her parents aren't any better than ours."

My only sin had been trusting the wrong person. Blaine Ashford's sin had been rape. And yet I had to leave my goddamn planet for another. Talk about some bullshit. I send another mental middle finger back to all those pretentious fucks on Earth and I wish for each and every single one of them to get a horrible case of gonorrhea.

A hard jarring movement sends shooting pain through me and almost pulls me back into consciousness, but I'm not ready to stop talking to Amelia, so I keep my eyes tightly shut and push all other thoughts away except her initial request.

"Why do you want me to stop fighting back?"

"Because he's coming," she replies cryptically.

"Who's coming?"

I'm jarred again and Amelia's form flickers.

"No, you can't go yet." It's a demand. "*Who's* coming?"

She flickers again and I cry out. It doesn't do any good. I'm jerked so hard, she's ripped from my mind. My eyes pop open right before I hit the ground. I'm not sure what hurts more, my head where the bastard yanked my hair or my ass from landing on it. "Goddamn it, you fucking shithead."

Casper jumps off his beast and lands easily on his feet. He stares down at me with those creepy demon eyes and evil smirk. I clench my fists and tense my muscles, prepared to junk punch him, but Amelia's words echo inside my head. Instead I slam my hands onto the dirt between my legs and scream out my frustration. Yellow-orange dust explodes up and hits me right in the face. I sputter and cough it out and the asshole and all his cronies—who've also dismounted—laugh.

"Fuck off." I gingerly climb to my feet—a task made difficult by the tether around my ankles—and glare at our surroundings, not sure why we've stopped.

While I was unconscious we've moved to a place in the forest where the trees have thinned out. In fact, it appears as though we're on flat land. And the grass has shifted shades. It's not so much yellow anymore, but more of an orange. Through a break in the trees, there's a large lake spread out to the left and my mouth waters at the thought of quenching my thirst. Aside from a couple brief stops to drink and relieve themselves, they've been riding hard, no doubt to put as much distance between us and the Tavikhi as they can.

Since we've stopped, I assume they feel confident no one will catch up to us. The ten males set up camp while my least favorite guy pushes me toward them. I stumble on my weakened legs and barely keep myself from falling flat on my face. I can't tell if this is the same jerk who showed up at the village three months ago or not. With their snow-white skin, bald heads, and red demon-eyes, all these assholes look the same to me. Except the one with the egg-shaped head. His noggin looks like it had been shat out by some chicken. I snort at the image.

My captor demands something that's pure gibberish to my ears with a jab of his finger toward the fire that's barely caught flame.

"I don't know what you're saying."

He repeats what's clearly a command with a none too gentle shove. The other ten dudes stop what they're doing and stare.

If my hands were untied, I'd slam them against my hips. I settle for tossing them over my head. "Can't you get it through your thick skull? I don't understand you. How many times do I have to say it before you figure it out, you dumbass?"

He moves so fast, I don't have time to dodge the blow. My head whips to the side and I lose my footing. A snapping sound hits my ears before the pain registers. "Mother *fucker*."

I curl into a fetal position and cradle my bound wrists against my chest as the tears fall and spots dance behind my closed lids. For people who want women, they sure don't know how to treat us.

"No wonder all your women fucked off if you kept slapping them around, you giant cock-wad." The words come out garbled between my clenched teeth. "If you weren't such a chicken shit and had to tie me up, I'd have gotten the hell out of here too. Your company leaves a lot to be desired."

Harsh voices and a sharp nudge to my back is the last straw.

I'm sorry, Amelia. I really did try. Hopefully, I'll see you soon. With that I release an inhuman scream, ignore the excruciating pain, scramble to my feet, and charge head-first into the cocksucker who I'm pretty sure just broke my arm.

CHAPTER 4

KYLER

Mellenje scatter from the trees and take to the sky as a primal scream rips through the air. Complete and utter silence follows. Not even the breeze blows to disturb the leaves around us. I exchange glances with the Krijese male on one side of me and with Katem on the other.

"Christ on a cracker, that sounds like Zara." Remi's voice shakes and she adjusts her grip on her sword.

Zydon's tail wraps around her waist and his gaze scans the forest.

"I believe it came from this direction." Kala points his war axe. His tracking skills are as good as, if not better than, any of ours.

There's only a brief glance between us all before we take off again. I don't wait for Remi to climb onto Zydon's back before I'm bounding from limb to limb high above the ground with my other tribe brothers keeping pace with me. Kala and the two Krijese race along the ground at an almost unnatural speed. They're not quite as fast as Tavikhi are when we swing from branch to branch, but they're certainly faster than us when traveling by foot.

Even though there are nine of us, it is most likely we will be outnumbered by the Njeri. We can only hope we're enough to defeat them before they get any closer to their village. It has been two turns of the sun since the attack on our people. Two turns since they took my—*the*—female. We've been on the move since. None of us have slept. Not even Remi, which caught me by surprise. But she is a strong female.

What had been more surprising is the Krijese's presence. Shortly after the start of the cold season, Kala's son Sorin had grown deathly ill. Desperate, he brought him to our village for healing. Sage saved the young kit's life. In return, Kala swore an oath of repayment to her. His presence, as well as that of his two tribe brothers, has seen the debt paid.

The sound of raised voices grows louder, and up ahead, light filters through the trees indicating they have thinned. I do not slow until I reach the last one. Katem and the other warriors stop as well and below me I catch a flash of movement from the Krijese before they halt as well. Just ahead, before the tree line ends and a large field opens up, are eleven Njeri arguing amongst themselves. My heart stops at the sight of the small female body lying unmoving at their feet.

A sharp inhalation comes from a nearby tree but is quickly cut off. Since no Tavikhi would make a sound, I can only assume it was Remi. I cast a glance to either side of me and the warriors more versed in battle send a silent message to each other. Katem nods in my direction and points at the circle of Njeri. They have not appeared to have sensed our presence yet.

I nod in return and from the sheath slung across my chest, I withdraw the sword at my back and wait with impatience. My tail remains tense and tightly looped around the nearest branch, ready to push off and propel my body toward our enemies and the female. When one Njeri makes a move toward Zara and reaches for her, I can no longer wait. He will *not* touch my female again.

With a roar that echoes around me, I launch myself out of the trees and onto the ground. I land roughly, but roll to my feet and charge forward, trusting my tribe brothers, sister, and the Krijese to do the same. Perhaps I am being reckless, but a force greater than me is ruling my choices. My opponent is the one who tried to touch Zara. Something tells me he is the reason she lies on the ground.

The Njeri and I battle.

I have a vague awareness of fighting all around me, but my entire focus is on the male in front of me. I will not let anything distract my need to kill. This is a new feeling rushing through me. Since I was a kit, I have only ever felt the need to help and heal. But the instinct to protect the female lying not far from where I defend her is stronger than anything I have ever known.

"You are weak, Tavikhi," the Njeri taunts me with an evil grin as he strikes hard against my sword.

I do not let his words bother me. Instead, I return the blow with one of my own and before he can recover, I land another. We trade hits, neither of us drawing blood until I spot an opening. A line of blood appears across his side, and he hisses in pain. I use it to my advantage and swing my sword hard and fast, first in one direction then the other causing him to retreat several steps. I twist slightly and use my tail to sweep his feet out from beneath him.

He collapses to the ground and I drive my blade through his chest, pinning him to the dirt. I stand over him and push my sword even harder downward, hatred giving me strength.

"Kyler," a panicked female voice calls out.

I yank my weapon from the Njeri's body and spin toward Remi. She kneels next to Zara, who still has not appeared to have woken. I rush over and drop to my knees beside them, trusting my tribe brothers to watch my back while I tend Zara.

"She won't wake up, and there's something wrong with her arm." Remi carefully pushes the bari-colored hair off her tribe sister's face.

One side of it is as dark as the color of the fiku trees, and her lips are swollen and crusted with dried blood. Her hands are bound tightly together, and a length of rope tethers her ankles as well. Most concerning is the odd angle in which her arm is bent. I glance at Remi.

"I need several branches at least this long and this wide." I use my hands to demonstrate. "I also need water."

Remi nods and takes off running. The sounds of battle dwindle until only harsh breathing remains. I grab my dagger from the belt at my waist and cut the bindings around Zara's ankles, and taking as much care as possible, from around her wrists. My fingers brush across her skin and a sharp jolt stings the tips of them. Right behind it is a burning sensation that travels upward. My gaze darts to the dark lines slowly appearing. My chest burns as well, but I do not need to look to know mating marks decorate it.

Emotions powerful enough to overwhelm sweep through me, but Zara moans and I push all of them away to focus on my mate. My *mate.*

"You are safe now, Zara," I rush to reassure her. "I will do everything in my power to take care of you and protect you. No one will harm you ever again."

Her eyes slowly open and meet mine. "*You.*"

That is all she says before she closes them again. I stare a moment longer. What did she mean it is me? Was she expecting me? Did she know I would come for her?

"By Deeka's flame." A shadow is cast over the ground beside Zara and me.

"No way." Remi drops to her knees again next to me with hands full of branches.

Zydon kneels beside her with a vessel of water. He scans

the marks lining my body. Without a word, I take the wood from the female and then carefully lift Zara's arm.

"I am sorry for the pain I am going to cause." Saying a quick prayer to Deeka, I jerk the bone into its proper position. Despite being unconscious, my mate screams and her entire frame jerks as she tries to rip her limb from my grip. I hold tight until she collapses, and then, using the sticks and sinew from the pouch at my waist, splint the break as best I can. Once I have secured it, I pour some burim root into the vessel and tend to the rest of her wounds.

While I work, Katem, Evren, Rassim, and the Krijese work on disposing of the Njeri. Remi and Zydon remain close by. Their whispered words reach me while I tend my mate, but I pay little attention. Within my chest, my soul light shines brightly and warms me from the inside out. Peace and contentment settle deep in my bones. Is this what it feels like to be mated? It is the most wondrous sensation.

Once Zara's face is cleaned of all the blood, I take a moment to study her. I do not know her age, but she is many cold seasons younger than me. When she awakens, will she be disappointed her mate is one of the older members of the tribe? The youngest elder is only eight warm seasons older than me. I am not a battle-worn warrior. I am, in fact, one of the leanest Tavikhi males in the entire tribe. Will Zara be disappointed by that as well?

"I can't believe she's your mate." Remi is careful of Zara's wounds as she strokes her hair. "She's never said it out loud, but I know she's been nervous about being alone since it's been months since the last human-Tavikhi mating."

Hearing Zara also was worried about ever finding a mate soothes something inside me. Humans do not have mates like Tavikhi do, so to know she has been hopeful for one makes my chest swell. "She will never be alone again now that she has me."

Kala approaches. His gaze lands on my mating marks and an emotion sparks in his dark eyes but quickly vanishes. "Ortak and I will scout ahead and make sure no Njeri are close by," he announces. "Their beasts will head back to their village and without riders, the other warriors will be alerted something is wrong and come to investigate."

I nod and the two males disappear into the trees on the opposite side of the clearing where our party stands. After a quick prayer to Deeka they do not find anything, I glance down at Zara. Pain and fatigue line her face. Her lips, cleared of blood, are cracked and dry. I soak the corner of a cloth in the burim-dosed water and drip the liquid into her mouth. She will need the pain medicine for when she awakens. It is unclear if she has suffered any other wounds besides the visible ones.

A dark rage rises from my belly that the Njeri may have hurt her in other ways. While they travelled fast, there has still been plenty of time for the males to have caused more damage to her. Damage I cannot see. *Please wake up.* I need to know where Zara has been hurt so I may make it go away. I shoot a glance over at the dead Njeri. I only wish I had been able to make his death slower and more painful.

My mate releases a moan and slowly stirs. Remi shifts and goes on alert. Zara's eyes open a fraction before widening farther. They land on me. I do not dare breathe as I wait for her reaction to the mating marks that have fully crept up my arms and chest. Her mouth opens and closes like a peshku gasping for breath on the banks of the water.

"I'm dead, aren't I?" she asks, her voice filled with pain.

"You are not dead."

"Are you sure?" Zara moves slightly and groans. "Okay, maybe you're right. No deity is cruel enough to make death hurt this fucking bad."

"Where do you hurt?" If I could take each of her pains into my own body I would.

She laughs lightly, but it swiftly changes to a moan. "The question is, where don't I? My arm is killing me. So's my face. My ribs and gut ache so bad if I had any food in it, I'd be barfing all over you." She winces. "Sorry."

"Do not be sorry." I grab the vessel from beside me. "Drink this. It should help."

Carefully, I tip the water into Zara's mouth. She swallows and then gags. "God, that tastes like shit."

I have drunk burim root many times but never thought it tasted like excrement. Bitter, yes. But not like waste. "It will help with the pain."

She drinks more but then turns her head away. "Okay, that's enough."

"Man, they really did a number on you, didn't they?" Remi lightly strokes Zara's forehead.

"You should see the other guy," she jokes and then tries to lift her head. With a pained groan she lowers it and closes her eyes. "If I'm not dead, I assume those bastards are?"

"Yes. You are safe," I assure her, not wanting her to be afraid.

"Good."

Just then, Kala and the other Krijese return.

"There is no sign of any Njeri, but we would be wise to start back to your village in case they are not far behind."

I shift my gaze to Zara, who is still pale. Travel is going to be difficult for her. She will not be able to ride on my back like Remi has done with Zydon. I also am not sure what to make of the fact she has not mentioned my mating marks. Perhaps she is in too much pain to have noticed.

Or perhaps she is trying to deny they exist.

CHAPTER 5

ZARA

The pain is making me delusional and I don't want everyone to know I'm losing my mind so I'm not going to ask if Kyler has mating marks. He sure didn't have them on whatever day these Njeri assholes took me from the village. They can't be because of me. There's no way the Deeka goddess chick is going to pair up a dude like the healer who has his shit together with the hot mess express that is Zara Black.

Weren't you the one who told Sage not so long ago the goddess doesn't make mistakes?

Shut up. No one asked you.

See? A delusional hot mess express who both talks to and answers herself.

"As much as this is going to suck, Kala's right. It's a long way back to the village, and god only knows if there are more Njeri heading this way," Remi says. "We don't want to get caught out here with no reinforcements if we need it."

Man, this really *is* going to suck. My entire body is killing me and I have zero energy. I've already caused everyone so many problems by getting snatched in the first place. I shift to try and push myself upright, but a lightning bolt hits and I grab Remi's arm. "Wait, are the girls okay? The guys?"

"They're fine. Worried about you, of course." She smiles, but it dims. "We did lose some people though—Tavikhi and human—and there's several more who still may not make it."

Damn it. More anger bubbles up and I half turn onto my good side to get my elbow underneath for leverage to sit up. An arm cradles my shoulder and back and I dart a quick glance sideways. My eyes meet yellow ones with a feline-like vertical pupil a purple so deep and dark to appear black. A jolt, almost like a shot of electricity zings through me, and my skin tingles as if it's hovering over live wire. This is as up close and personal as I've ever been to one of the Tavikhi warriors, and it just so happens to be the guy I'm hallucinating has mating marks.

"Careful." His warm, husky voice sends heat straight to my lady parts and my cheeks turn to fire.

I dip my head in barely a nod, cradle my arm against my chest, and let Kyler help me to my feet. It's slow going, and the pain is so excruciating I have to grit my teeth, but I finally make it. Except the minute I'm fully upright, dizziness hits. I sway and frantically blink to try and keep myself from passing out. The scent of eucalyptus—which should smell medicinal but doesn't—along with a hint of some kind of sweet fragrance filters into my consciousness as I breathe it in deeply. It actually somehow helps to center my awareness and I send a grateful smile to the male keeping me from falling over. At the same time I try to put some space between us because being this close to the healer is doing things to my body.

"Thanks. I think I'm okay now." God, how embarrassing.

What might be disappointment flashes across Kyler's face, but it quickly disappears. "If you would rather someone else assist you, I understand."

I jerk slightly and wince as pain shoots through my arm. Nausea clenches my belly as well. "No, it's fine. I just needed a second."

"If you are certain."

Why is *he* the one who doesn't sound certain? "I appreciate your help."

Kyler reaches into his satchel. "Then may I bind your arm to you? It will provide support."

He brings out a length of leather and with a gentle touch, creates a sling I can rest my arm in. I try desperately to ignore his closeness and the way his breath caresses my ear as he ties it behind my neck. A shiver I can't stop runs down my spine, and the hairs on my forearms stand on end. Kyler's gaze drops to my mouth, and I realize I'm biting my bottom lip. I release it and take a step back. His eyes shutter and a pinch of guilt hits me.

Acutely aware of everyone staring at us, I take tentative steps toward the forest in the direction I think the village lies. Each one sends a small jolt of pain through my throbbing arm. I drank almost an entire cup of nasty ass water. How much more could I be hurting if I hadn't? I have a feeling I'll find out before we get back to the village.

Kyler has released his hold on me, but he remains so close while we walk we're practically touching. So much heat radiates off him, my side is almost sweating. I take a closer look at our small party. I'm shocked to find three Krijese speaking quietly amongst themselves. My guess is Sage had something to do with their presence. I might have to actually hug her as a thank you.

Who I'm not shocked to see is Zydon. Not with Remi here. I knew she'd come. I'm closest to Maeve, but Remi and I have the most in common, being from the upper tier, and shitty, rich parents who didn't give a fuck about us. She's the one who helped me see I'm not completely useless despite my upbringing. Although considering my only skill—and it's barely even one at that—is making tolerable arrowheads, I'm not really sure I'm that useful either.

I'm thankful for the other Tavikhi who joined the group. Not just because they rescued me, but because it means they're still alive. My heart aches that some of the villagers were killed. While I tend to stick close to my friends or hang out in the forge, every Tavikhi I've encountered has treated me with respect, as if I'm one of them. It's been nice to be part of something like a large, extended family.

I glance at Kyler again and scan his torso and arms. Yep, they're still there. I really need to get Remi alone for a second and talk to her. I'm so distracted by his mating marks, I miss whatever it is I trip over. Bracing myself for a world of hurt, I wait for the agony. Except it never comes.

A heavy weight lies around my waist and brings me upright until I'm steady on my feet. I glance down to find Kyler's tail wrapped around me. My gaze jerks up to meet his. He's so close. The marks on his skin darken a shade, which I've only ever seen happen on a newly mated male. Unbidden, I reach out and touch the swirling line running along his bicep. He sucks in a breath and his muscles twitch. He yanks his tail away from me and to my shock, I miss it.

I snatch my hand back and shuffle as quickly forward as my weakened body will let me. "Sorry."

"It is I who should apologize. I only meant to keep you from falling. It was not my intention to touch you without your consent," Kyler says stiffly already having caught up with me.

Okay. Something's not right here. I may not know the healer well, but I've been around him enough times in the nearly five months we've been on this planet to know he's a good guy. Confident. Kind. Friendly. He's never acted like this. At least not that I've ever seen. I dart a quick glance around. No one appears to be paying us any attention. They're all focused on the forest around us. No doubt checking for danger. So, here goes nothing.

"Have I done something to offend you?"

Kyler's head snaps in my direction and his eyes widen. "Not at all *kee*—Zara."

Holy shit on a stick. Had he just been about to call me *keeshla*? That's the word all the Tavikhi warriors use to refer to their fated mate. My mouth drops open. "Jesus H. You *do* have mating marks."

Fuck me. Is this who Amelia meant when she said 'he's coming'?

The healer's brow bones shift downward in the inner corners and he glances at his arms. "Can you not see them well?"

I step over a large root spread across the ground. Admitting to Kyler I thought I was hallucinating them makes me sound like an idiot. "Yeah, I see them fine," I mumble.

He opens his mouth, but snaps it shut. A weird and uncomfortable silence lingers. I let it remain as I keep walking, but the fatigue and weariness I've been trying to push away is growing stronger. We've barely gone anywhere, but I'm not sure how much farther I'm going to be able to go. As though sensing I'm at my limit, Kyler slows and then stops.

"We need to rest," he announces.

Kala glances behind us. "We have barely even traveled the length of your village. We must keep moving."

Kyler's expression hardens. "I said we are resting."

I lay my hand on his arm and a shock stings my finger. "It's okay. I can keep going."

He shakes his head. "No, you cannot. It is my job as the healer and as…your mate to take care of you. It is obvious you are struggling, and I will not have you injured more than you already are. We will make camp here until you have recovered your energy."

A funny little zing goes through my chest at hearing him call me his mate. Everyone murmurs to themselves, but to my surprise, no one argues again. Instead, they all move about the area and form a watchful perimeter around Kyler and me.

"Come, sit." He takes my arm and guides me to a large tree stump nearby. I try to ignore the tingling sensation rippling through my veins. Once seated, he removes something from the small satchel around his hips. "Eat. Slowly, though."

I take some dried meat from his hand and don't question what it is—at this point, I'll eat just about anything. Taking small bites, because I'm smart enough to know I might make myself sick otherwise, I nibble away at the piece of jerky. It's a little gamey, but the smoky flavor mostly covers it up. Once I've eaten more than half of it, Kyler passes me a vessel of water. A smidgen of guilt looms.

"Sorry. I drank almost all of it." I pass the nearly empty container back.

"Do not concern yourself." He waves away my apology. "We have more than enough."

I'll take his word for it. My stomach feels full, but it's still no doubt bruised and aches a bit. The pain in my arm is returning already as well. I'm such a pussy. "Do you have any more pain reliever?"

Kyler goes on high alert. "What hurts?"

Everything. But that's not really what he's asking. "My arm's aching again. Just something to take the edge off."

He reaches into his satchel and brings out a small leather pouch. I watch as he pours a small amount of a powder into the water and hands it over. Trying not to gag on the bitter taste, I take a few small drinks before I stop myself. My gut is water-logged. "Thanks."

While we continue resting, I finish off the remainder of the jerky. I'm nowhere near one hundred percent—hell, I doubt I'm at fifty—but I know how important it is we keep going. I've sensed the unease and impatience of the warriors. Even Remi's paced restlessly. I glance at Kyler. There's no way I want him to think I'm useless. Other than the single time he called me his mate, he hasn't brought it up again. He probably regrets getting saddled with me for the remainder of his life.

I mean, what do I have to bring to the relationship? I can't cook. I can't sew. Christ, I can barely fold a fur. What kind of mate am I going to be? A terrible kind, that's what. I should be trying to impress Kyler. Except I have zero skills. Which means, the least I can do is not be a baby.

"Thank you for letting me rest. I'm feeling better, so we should probably get going." I carefully stand and hope I don't get dizzy and fall over. When nothing happens, I breathe out a sigh of relief.

He studies me, and I do my best not to squirm under his penetrating gaze. I can tell he wants to argue but I rush to stop him. "Really, I'm okay. Or at least I will be. You know as well as I do we're not going to be safe until we get back to the village." Maybe not even then.

Finally, Kyler dips his head in agreement. "You will tell me when the pain and fatigue become too great. We *will* rest."

I nod. With slow steps I take off again and he moves right next to me for the second time, although there is barely enough room on the non-existent path for me to travel. Remi and Zydon, along with Katem, quicken their pace and take point, scouting the terrain in front of us. Evren, Rassim, and the three Krijese fall behind to watch our backs.

The forest is silent aside from the sound of mellenje and the scurrying of small creatures as they rush to get away from us. Sage hasn't talked a lot about Kyler, but from everything she has said, I never pictured him to be this quiet. Is it because of me? Granted, I always have something to say. Yet, I'm struggling to find any words. Is this how it's going to be between us? This awkward, uncomfortable silence that feels oppressive?

Fuck. Is this another Sage and Jodah situation? Does Kyler not feel the bond despite his mating marks? Is that why he isn't acting all love-sick and spouting on about how much Deeka has blessed him?

Son of a bitch.

CHAPTER 6

KYLER

For more than four lunar cycles, I have watched Zara and during none of them has she ever been this quiet. She is bold and always has something to say. There are warriors who fear Benham, our head warrior and weapon maker, even now that he's mated and has become slightly more approachable. Yet, even before Maeve triggered his mating marks, Zara bravely faced him without hesitation and asked to apprentice at his forge. She showed more courage than many of the young Tavikhi.

Remi closes the distance between her and Zara. My mate darts a glance in my direction. As much as I do not want to leave her side in case she needs me, I slow my pace and move slightly behind to give the two females a bit of privacy. Whispered words are exchanged between them and Remi's gaze shifts over her shoulder to me several times and each time, I meet it. I also try not to stare at my mate's backside, but I am far from successful. Where her tribe sister is tall and slender, Zara is much shorter with far more curves. If memory serves, she is only slightly taller than Maeve, who is the smallest of the females.

Finally, Remi breaks away and returns to Zydon's side. My steps quicken and in moments, I am walking next to my mate again. Even if she does not speak to me, I want to be close.

"Remi said that, after her, you were the first to volunteer to come get me." Zara surprises me by breaking the silence between us.

"Yes." There is no reason to deny it.

A long pause follows my response. "Did you know then?"

"Did I know what?"

Zara swallows. "That I was your mate?"

I had not expected to be asked such a thing. There should not be any lies between us though. As much as I am uncertain how my *keeshla* feels, I cannot hide myself from her. "No."

She nods.

"But I had hoped."

Zara turns her head in my direction. Her eyes, with their dark smudges beneath, are wide. "You...hoped?"

"Yes."

A large fallen branch covers the path in front of us. I move even closer to assist her over it. Her breaths are labored from the steady upward trek through the hillside. To my great pleasure, she takes my hand without hesitation and climbs over the fiku limb. I leap over and we resume walking.

"Why?" Zara asks after several moments.

Why had I hoped? Does she not realize any male would be lucky to call himself her mate?

"Is it because I'm one of the few females left?" she asks before I can tell her my reason.

"Of course not."

Zara gives me the human gesture called a shrug. "I mean, I'd understand if I was just the last resort. I know you guys have been hurting for fated mates for years and a lot of you have given up on the idea you might find yours."

"That is not the case at all," I rush to assure her. "You are not a last resort. I have prayed to Deeka you were my mate almost from the moment you came to the village with the shefira and the rest of your tribe sisters."

No doubt I have now scared her.

"You have?" Zara's voice rises in disbelief. "But...but why? I don't understand."

"It is not something I can explain. From the instant I saw you there has been something pulling at me. A need of some kind." It never lessened. "Of course, it was only wishful thinking. I am nearly an elder. You are a young female, and there are many young warriors. One of whom I was certain Deeka had chosen as your mate."

"I see."

I glance over at her. There was a tone to her words I cannot interpret. Was it disappointment? "I know I am probably not the kind of mate you would wish for yourself, but—"

"What kind of mate do you think I wish for exactly?" Zara cuts me off so abruptly I actually startle.

Her question makes me pause. Although it is not so much the question itself, but rather the sharp tone in which she asked it. "I merely assumed you would want someone who is much closer to your age. A warrior. You have an interest in weapon making. It is something you and a mate would have in common. I fight when I must, but it is not where my skills or true passion lies."

For several beats she does not speak. "Maybe I'm not the kind of mate you'd wish for," Zara finally says softly.

How can she believe that? Unwillingly, words spill from my lips. "You are everything I would wish for in a mate."

For a second time, she stumbles, and I clasp her with my tail to keep her upright. "Are you all right? Do we need to rest again?"

She waves me off. "Thanks, I'm fine. Really."

Taking her at her word, I loosen my tail. This time, I am much slower to remove it from around her waist and when her fingers accidentally brush across its length, a shudder runs through me. Have I spoken too boldly? I am at a loss as to how to talk to Zara. No female has made me as uncertain as she. I glance at the males and Remi surrounding us. They are alert, with weapons drawn and ready to protect us.

My gaze lands on Kala. His mate was struck down by a disease many seasons ago. I have no knowledge of his two tribe brothers, but with the few female Krijese that belong to their village, I suspect they are unmated as well. Of the Tavikhi with our party, only Zydon and Rassim are mated. Rassim and Alanda were one of the last fated mate pairings to occur amongst our tribespeople. It is clear how much Zydon and Remi have in common, which gives them much to speak about. They are comfortable with each other.

They were not always that way. Yes, this is something I must remind myself of. There was much conflict between Remi and Zydon at the beginning. I do not want there to be any between Zara and me. I must learn how to talk to her. If she is not going to be bold, then I must.

"From the time I was a kit, I have wished for a mate. A blessed gift from Deeka. No matter how much time passed, the wish remained. Even when season after season passed and no new mated pairs appeared, I never gave up hope." I have trusted the goddess to lead my path. "Throughout the seasons, I have imagined the traits my mate will carry. She is, above all things, kind. She is generous. A loyal and trustworthy friend. She laughs often. She is someone who I can picture waking up with every morning and lying beside every night. From the beginning, I had hoped Deeka put you in my path because you are all of those things."

I glance over at Zara. I am not sure what reaction I expect, but tears are not it. They glisten in her eyes and slide down her cheeks. She sniffs and swipes them away. Sage has told me of the wetness that leaks from humans. It is often a sign of sorrow, but it can also signify happiness. Except I am unsure what they mean coming from my mate.

"Have I said too much? I know humans do not have a soul light to bond them to their mate, so I do not expect you to have similar feelings. But I do not ever want you to question what you mean to me. Not as just some female, but what *you*, Zara from Earth, mean. I know without any uncertainty no other female would do. You were meant to be mine. If Deeka had not brought you here, then I would have died alone."

The tears have increased and spill from her eyes at a speed faster than she is able to wipe them away.

"I am sorry if I have upset you."

Zara comes to an abrupt halt and whirls on me with her good hand fisted at her side. "Stop apologizing. Stop acting like there's something wrong with you. And stop being so fucking nice."

Before I can process her demands, she blinks once, twice, and then collapses. With far quicker reflexes than I knew I possessed, I catch her before she hits the ground.

"Zara," Remi calls out and rushes over.

As gently as possible, I lay my mate on the forest floor. Her cheeks have lost some of their color, and the dark smudges under her eyes have grown darker. She is breathing, but I fear her breaths are far too shallow. Or perhaps it is only my poor imagination. Other than her broken arm and the dried blood and discoloration on her face, she does not display any other outward injuries. Is there some hurt inside her I cannot see?

Never have I felt the terror I do at the thought of being unable to heal my mate. I take a deep breath and push away the fear and uncertainty. Neither will do Zara any good.

"I need more water." Taking a small fur from my satchel, I place it under her head.

Carefully, I check the splint on her arm and confirm it is still secure. There is some swelling, but nothing to concern me at the moment. I bring out the small pouch of burim root and add it to the water I still have left. Remi hands me another vessel and I put a bit of eshe in it to help with keeping a fever at bay.

Zara's eyes flutter and then slowly open. "Shit, what happened?" she asks weakly.

"You passed out. That's what happened," Remi announces before I can. "We're done moving for the day. You need to recover."

My mate has proven to be a bit stubborn, so it surprises me when she offers no argument but instead nods and closes her eyes. I am glad she is listening to her tribe sister, although if Remi had not forced the issue, I would have.

Stopping so close to where we battled the Njeri is not the best thing to do, but my only concern is my mate's health. She is in no shape to travel any farther today.

She opens her eyes and they meet mine. "Sorry I was such a bitch."

The word bitch does not translate, but I understand her apology. "Perhaps both of us should stop apologizing."

Zara gives me a weak smile. "Yeah, perhaps."

I help her sit upright and pick up the burim-infused water. "Why don't you drink this? It will help with your pain."

She grimaces but finishes the remaining liquid.

"And some of this." I offer the other vessel.

Zara mumbles something about piss beneath her breath, but she swallows several mouthfuls before passing the container back. "I'm going to drown if you keep giving me all this water."

I bite back my grin. It is good to hear the spark of annoyance in her voice. It is much better than the pain or uncertainty. This is the Zara I am used to. The one who shows her fire. The one who sets my blood and body aflame.

CHAPTER 7

I wasn't joking when I said I'm going to drown. Already my gut is waterlogged and despite being dehydrated, I suspect I'm going to have to pee shortly. Something I'm not looking forward to, considering I'm currently handicapped. Thank god for Remi, although I doubt she pictured having to help me drop trou when she joined this little rescue mission. I've never been particularly shy about being naked in front of girlfriends, but this is pushing the boundaries of friendship.

"I'm sor—"

Kyler shakes his head and places a finger over my lips, halting my words. "No more apologies, remember?"

I nod, trying—and failing—to ignore the tingle running across my skin at his touch. What would other parts of me feel like if he touched them too? A heat blooms deep within me and I almost cry out from the loss when he lowers his hand.

"Zydon and I are going hunting," Remi announces. "You good?"

I turn to her. "I'm good."

She gives me a knowing smirk and walks over to her mate, leaving me alone with mine. She and Zydon disappear into the trees before I remember I'm probably going to need her help before they get back. Shit. The remaining warriors give the two of us a wide berth while they make camp. My stomach rumbles again. Kyler reaches into his satchel and brings out more jerky.

"Thank you." I hope Remi and Zydon bring back something with a bit more substance. This will do for the moment, but if I'm going to walk the rest of the way back to the village, I need fuel.

I nibble on the meat and wonder where the hell the Zara who stood in front of grouchy Benham only a few months ago and basically told him she was working with him went? Or the Zara who spent an entire year needling Clifton and Priscilla at every opportunity? She needs to make a reappearance. Taking a deep breath, I meet Kyler's eyes. Not that it's hard to do considering he hasn't taken them off me since I came to.

"So...fated mates, huh?" Mentally, I smack my forehead. What a dumbass thing to say. Of course we are, otherwise, his mating marks wouldn't be present.

One side of his mouth kicks up and my lady parts stand at attention at the dimple that appears. "Fated mates."

"Cool. Cool." Another mental smack. *Jesus*. I take a deep breath. "I mean, wow. You and me? Who'd have thought?"

That's not any better. Where's the hole in the ground to swallow me when I need it? Thankfully, Kyler's smile only widens.

"It would appear Deeka did."

I chuckle. "Yeah, I guess she did."

To my surprise, an easy silence falls. "I can't remember if I've even said thank you. For coming after me."

"What kind of mate would I have been if I had not?"

"Except you didn't know I was your mate at the time," I remind Kyler.

His gaze grows distance before he blinks and looks at me. "Deeka knew. No doubt it was she who guided me to you."

I've always believed in a higher power—even if I rejected it after Amelia was gone—so accepting the fact some goddess gave him the push to come after me isn't difficult. "You're probably right. Still, thank you for listening to her."

"Always."

I adjust my arm within the sling, wincing slightly at the

throbbing just beneath the surface. "Do you know this is the first bone I've ever broken?"

"You have been lucky then," Kyler says.

"More like I was kept on a tight leash."

His brow bones shift. An action I wouldn't have said was sexy until now. "What is a leash?"

I curse my stupid mouth. No one wants to spill their childhood trauma to a guy they hardly know. We may have been living in the same village for the last four months, and we are obviously now mates, but he and I are most definitely not *there* yet. Then again, if we're going to be spending our lives together, it's only fair Kyler know what he's in for having me as his wifey.

"It's like a tether."

His feline-like eyes widen, then narrow, and there's a sudden tension in his body. His fists clench. "They tether humans on Earth?"

Of course the concept doesn't translate. Tavikhi wouldn't understand the dynamics back home. "Not literally. It's a figure of speech. It just means I wasn't allowed a lot of opportunities to do any activities that could lead to broken bones."

Kyler blinks and cocks his head slightly. His mouth parts as though he has more questions, and I brace myself for whatever they might be. There must be an expression on my face that gives him pause, because his lips close.

"I had really controlling parents." Might as well lay all the facts out there.

It's not as though the girls don't know my history. Most of it anyway. Only Maeve knows about Amelia. Well, maybe Sage. I didn't ask, and she's never mentioned it.

A warm hand covers mine. "I am sorry you were not given the freedom to experience things."

Freedom.

I suppose in some ways I was a prisoner. Although, what normal person would complain about being given every advantage in life? My closet had been full of more clothes than I could wear in a lifetime. Same with shoes. If I wanted something, I never had to worry about not having enough credits. Compared to the bottom tier, I had access to anything I could ever want. But what does that matter if, at the same time, I was slowly being suffocated? Smothered and controlled to the point that I had almost no autonomy. It's only one of the reasons I rebelled so hard.

I squeeze Kyler's hand and don't let go. His touch is comforting, which is even more shocking since I'm not really one for showing affection. Not since Amelia. "Thank you."

We sit there for several minutes, neither of us letting the other go. When was the last time I did nothing more than hold someone's hand? I'm not sure I ever have. My sister most likely, but it's been so long since she's been gone, my memories aren't reliable. Every time Bryce touched me, I had to withhold my flinch. I didn't want to be labeled a freak. Fat lot of good that did me.

The quiet of the forest, along with Kyler's presence, is soothing. The warriors who stayed behind talk softly amongst themselves, although Kala and Evren are missing. Considering the Krijese's warning about not staying put for long, he's probably out scouting for more Njeri. For the first time in a long time, a small amount of peace settles over me. At least until a sudden urge hits out of nowhere. Mother fu…

C'mon, not now, damn it. Except my body is betraying me. I press my thighs together and clench to try and keep the need at bay, but it's not doing shit.

"Is all well, Zara?" Kyler shifts closer as if he might need to rush to my aid.

Fuck.

I have two choices. One, I can embarrass myself by pissing my pants or two, I can embarrass myself by having him help me to nature's toilet. Neither choice is appealing, but if I'm going to be mortified, I'd rather be mortified with dry pants. Plus, as my mate, Kyler's going to see my undercarriage one of these days anyway. Might as well be today.

I clear my throat. God, could my life get any worse? I hastily glance up and stare at the canopy of trees as though the deity lives within them. *No, wait, forget I said anything.* I turn my head to the male beside me and blow out a heavy breath.

"All the water I drank needs somewhere to go." I raise my arm a fraction and pray I'm spared the indignity of asking for assistance by the sudden appearance of Remi, but no such luck. "I'm…I'm going to need some help though. Please."

For a second, I worry I'll have to spell it out even farther, but Kyler's eyes pop open. He scrambles to his feet and stretches out a hand. Avoiding eye contact, I clasp it and let him help me up.

"Come this way." He leads me away from our camp and deeper into the trees.

Forest sounds remain and the cool air feels good against my heated cheeks. Despite the thick overgrowth, I can tell it's late in the day. A slight breeze blows the branches so they sway and dance, exposing fragments of the darkening sky. I get a few flashes of one of the moons. Soon, it's going to be too dark to see anything in front of my face.

We don't travel far when Kyler comes to a stop and faces me. "What do you need me to do?"

"Just stand here for a second, please." I work at my pants, but the urge grows stronger and I'm far too slow. "Goddamn it. I can't get these off."

I don't have to ask twice. In a flash, my pants and underwear are down around my knees. I grab his arm to steady myself and squat. Because this whole thing isn't bad enough, I start humming to cover up the sound and if there's one thing I'm not, it's someone who can sing on-key for shit.

For another minute I stay in position until I use my legs to push myself to standing. Except my weakened muscles scream in protest. I'm stuck right where I am. With my cooch nearly touching the ground and a puddle of piss beneath me while I hold onto a hot dude for dear life so I don't fall on my bare ass.

It's so absolutely ridiculous that a snort escapes. Then a small chuckle, until I'm laughing so hard tears fall. Except the laughter dries up, and all I'm left with are tears of mortification. I'm sobbing so hard, I barely notice Kyler brings me to my feet, redresses me, and picks me up. I'm cradled in his arms, with my head on his shoulder. He carries me back to camp and sits on a stump with me in his lap. He holds me until I'm all cried out. Even then, I don't move.

I breathe in his sweet eucalyptus fragrance and soak in his warmth. The fact I'm not ready to clamber off him doesn't escape me. If it were anyone else, I'd be itching to get away from their touch. It makes me twitchy. But not Kyler's. If his mating marks didn't signify we were mates, this cements it.

Finally, I wipe away the dried tracks on my cheeks and raise my head to meet his gaze. I'm so close I can make out the tiny furrows at the corners of his eyes and above his brow bones, as well as the various strands of white hairs threaded through the yellow-gold ones. Has Sage ever mentioned Kyler's age before? He said he's almost an elder, but other than the few lines on his face, I never would have guessed.

Some compulsion moves me to reach up and trace them. He freezes beneath my touch and his vertical pupils dilate.

An acute awareness passes between us, and the surrounding forest and people disappear. The throbbing ache in my core returns, and as though he can scent my arousal, Kyler's nostrils flare.

Without thinking I lean in and brush my lips across his. Up until the humans got here, this intimate act isn't something the Tavikhi did. They'd never heard of kissing before so they started calling it mouth touching, which always makes me smile. A noise breaks us apart and Kyler's hand goes to the sword strapped across his back, but he lowers it at the sight of Zydon and Remi returning. Each carries a dreri over their shoulders.

Her gaze scans the camp until it lands on me. One side of her mouth kicks up and heat returns to my face at the position I'm in. Refusing to be embarrassed for where I'm seated, I wiggle my eyebrows up and down. She chuckles and shakes her head. I turn back to Kyler.

"Thank you. For taking care of me." No one's cared for me since Amelia died except myself. It's actually kind of nice to let someone else do it for a change.

Don't get used to it, since it probably won't last.

"You are my mate. It is not only my duty, but rather, my privilege, to care for you," Kyler says with an intense stare.

I shift under the scrutiny and then abruptly freeze at the hardness beneath my ass. An impish part of me wants to torture him just a little, but I'll be torturing myself as well. We're out in the open and surrounded by people. Neither of us can act on the obvious attraction between us. But also, I'm injured and not in the best shape to be getting frisky, even if I wanted to. Not that I don't want to, but I can admit being terrified. The last time I was with someone, my life went tits up and I wound up here.

"Thank you," I repeat rather lamely.

The smell of a fire reaches me, and I carefully make to stand. Kyler helps me to my feet and I can sense his hesitation before he releases his hold. Together we walk over to where everyone is gathering. Rassim and Katem are skinning the two dreri. Kala and Evren still haven't returned, but I suspect they'll be here soon. The two Krijese are getting a fire going, while Zydon and Remi spread out a fur.

Like always, I feel useless. I should be helping. Or at least trying.

"You need to rest," Kyler says and guides me close to the fire. He helps me to sit. "Do you need more pain reliever?"

I shake my head. I don't want to appear weak. "Not at the moment, thanks."

"Will you be all right while I assist Rassim and Katem?"

"Of course." There's no reason for him to babysit me when I'm just sitting here. Besides, I need time alone to think about that kiss. It barely qualified as one, but I'm still feeling the urge to squirm and ease the ache deep inside.

Kyler takes a long look at me before nodding. To my shock, he palms the back of my neck and kisses me hard.

The pleasure barely registers, and he's gone. I sit there in stunned silence with my fingers pressed against my lips and watch him walk away with his tail thrashing madly behind him. A slow smile curls my lips as the thought of all the things that tail might do to me once I'm healed.

CHAPTER 8

KYLER

I have watched every human-Tavikhi mated couple mouth touch, and each time, a wild curiosity has risen inside me to experience this thing they call kissing for myself. Nothing could have prepared me for the swift arousal that hit at the feel of Zara's lips against mine.

How could something as simple as touching my mouth to another being cause such a riot of sensations? Yet, the exact moment she kissed me, I had grown rock hard. All I want to do is take her to my furs and taste every bit of flesh, especially between her thighs. My tongue aches with the need to know her flavor. The scent of her cunt lingers in my nose, the air thick and musky with Zara's arousal.

I adjust myself beneath my leg coverings. A dampness remains from the mating fluid leaking out of my cock nodes. It is an uncomfortable sensation, but I ignore it as I assist Katem and Rassim with skinning the dreri. I must provide for my mate. While I work, I keep watch in case she needs me, but Remi has joined her and the two of them sit together.

"Blessings on your mating," Rassim says. "Zara is a fine female."

Although he is already mated, a surge of possessiveness rises. Zara is *mine*. "Yes, she is."

Katem is silent, and I cast my eyes in his direction. I cannot help but pity my tribe brother and the fact he does not have what Rassim and I do. There are several unmated females back in our village, both Tavikhi and human, but with every passing season the chances of one of them being the *keeshla* of a warrior lessens. My gaze travels back to Zara. Although, with six matings over the last nearly five lunar cycles, hope is returning to our people. Another ship from Terra may arrive soon, and with it...possibility.

I do not want to offer false wishes, but I send up a prayer to Deeka that she provides our unmated tribe brothers and sisters with their fated mate. Each of them is honorable and worthy of the happiness I feel. Soon, we have the dreri over the fire. Just as we finish setting them up, Kala and Evren return.

"Still no sign of any Njeri. We should be safe for the night," the Krijese announces.

By morning, I hope Zara is well enough to continue the journey back to the village. Once again, my gaze is drawn to her. However, Remi is no longer with her and she sits, alone, propped up against a tree with her good arm cradling the broken one. She adjusts it and winces. Our eyes meet and she gives me a small smile. I walk over and seat myself beside her.

"Is it time for more pain reliever?" I reach for my pouch, but Zara shakes her head.

"I'm okay. It just throbs a bit."

My gaze sharpens. "It is not weakness to take something for the pain. There is no need to suffer just to appear strong."

She laughs. "You don't have to worry about me. I'm a big baby and don't deal well with pain. I promise if it gets to be more than I can handle, I'll swallow more of that nasty shit you call medicine."

Taking her at her word, I lower my arm. We sit together in silence, observing the others. Zara opens her mouth and emits a sound. She lays her hand across her face to muffle it. "Sorry, I'm just a little tired. Who knew getting abducted was so exhausting?"

There is obvious humor in her tone, but beneath it I sense something deeper. Something more painful. It reminds me that I have not asked of any injuries that are not obvious. Shame fills me that I have not been a better healer or mate.

"The Njeri did not hurt you…" my voice trails off, unsure of how to ask the question that has been haunting me since we found Zara.

She turns her head toward me with a crease between her furry brows. I glance quickly down and back up. Her eyes widen and she rattles her head. "No, they didn't hurt me like that."

My body sags with relief and the tension bleeds from my clenched fists. "I am glad you did not suffer in that way. Death would have been too swift for them if they had."

A moment of silence settles between us.

"Someone hurt my sister like that a long time ago," Zara says so quietly I almost miss it. "I wish the guy who did it was dead instead of her."

I turn. She is staring straight ahead, and her eyes shimmer with unshed tears. In a blink, they disappear and she faces me. One side of her mouth curls up slightly, but it is not with humor. "Do you know, other than Maeve, you're the first person I've ever told that to?"

With great caution, I thread my fingers through hers. Warmth fills me that she does not withdraw. "You honor me with your trust, and I am sorry for the loss of your sister."

Zara shrugs. "It was a long time ago."

Gently, I squeeze her hand. "Time does not matter when it comes to grief. My family, including a brother, has been gone for many seasons, and I still mourn their passing. It often hurts to think of them, but I also work to remember all the good things about them. I know they would want that, and although I did not know your sister, I believe that if she is anything like you, she would want that as well."

Zara stares into my eyes and then leans forward to press a soft kiss against my lips. "Thank you for that. You're right.

Amelia wouldn't want me to wallow in grief for too long. Up until that day, she was always positive and cheerful. She was my best friend."

"She sounds like a wonderful sister."

"Yeah, she was the best."

There is a comfort in sitting quietly with someone that I have never experienced until this moment. Zara continues letting me hold her hand until finally, she shifts.

"I think I could use some of that pain medicine now," she admits.

"Of course." Once I have poured burim root into some water, I pass it over.

She drinks it and makes a sound of distaste when finished. "Good god, that stuff is awful. I don't know how you guys can handle it."

I chuckle. "It is certainly not the most tasteful."

"'Not the most tasteful'? Are you kidding? It tastes like shit rolled in shit covered in more shit." Zara exaggerates a shudder and gags.

"Since I do not know what excrement tastes like, I will have to take your word for it." Do humans eat excrement?

She laughs loudly and covers her mouth, unsuccessfully holding back the sound. "Saying something tastes like shit is just an expression. I don't actually know what it tastes like."

"That is good to hear. I wondered what sort of planet you came from where people ate waste."

"I mean, I'm sure there are humans that do eat it, but I'm definitely not one of them." Zara's humor is evident.

There is a sense of pride that I am able to make her laugh, even if it at a misunderstanding of her culture. Her smile is beautiful and I would love to see more of it. Especially as it feels as though I am seeing the real one. She smiles often in the village, but this one makes her entire being glow.

"The meat is ready," Katem calls out from next to the fire where Evren and Kala are removing the dreri from it.

"Come, let us eat." I stand and reach down to help my mate to her feet.

"Thanks." She releases me and brushes the dirt off the back of her leg coverings.

I try to quell the disappointment that she does not take my hand again as we walk to where everyone is gathered. One of the Krijese has made flat wood platters and Kala places several pieces of meat on each one that is then passed around until everyone has one. We all sit together around the flames to eat, except for Rassim and the two Krijese. The three of them take their food into the forest, no doubt to maintain watch. Although Kala and Evren did not see any evidence of Njeri, our enemies are not the only preda-tors that lurk in the trees.

"We are still two turns of the sun away from our village," Zydon says. "Tonight we must all rest and be ready to travel in the morning."

For some reason I bristle. Zara is not a Tavikhi warrior. She is a human female who is far more fragile than us.

"Calm, Kyler," he tells me. "I meant no disrespect to your mate."

To my surprise, and without realizing it, I have clenched my fists. A cool hand on mine releases the tension from me and I turn to find Zara touching me.

"It's okay. I know we need to get moving in case there's danger," she says. "Zydon is just reminding everyone what needs to be done so we're all safe."

I nod and she drops her arm to her side. I turn to my tribe brother. "Apologies."

Zydon dips his head in acceptance. Everyone returns to eating and the only sound is that of the forest around us. A breeze has stirred up and despite the fact warm season is upon us, there is a drop in temperature. It does not help that we are deep within the trees and minimal light from the moons is able to make it through the leaves. Soon, it will be too dark for the females to see and more difficult—although not impossible—for me and my tribe brothers.

Unlike the evening meals in the village where all the tribespeople gather for conversation and the kits run and play with each other, the atmosphere tonight is filled with tension and unease. We must remain vigilant and alert for danger. At last, after everyone has had their fill, we pack the remaining bits of dreri to hopefully sustain us until we reach our village. Zara rests her head against the tree behind her, and her breathing evens out.

I return to her side, and she jerks upright with wide eyes and a gasp.

"It is only I, *keeshla.*" The fear in her gaze makes me rage and wish I could kill the Njeri all over again, only this time more slowly.

She places her hand over her heaving chest and takes deep, calming breaths. "Guess I'm a little jumpy."

"That is understandable after what you have gone through. I did not mean to frighten you. If you do not mind, I will remain at your side through the night. No harm will come to you." This is my vow.

Zara does not respond for several beats, until finally, she nods. "I think I'd like that."

I scoot close enough that our legs and shoulders touch. Her skin is already chilled. Before the night is over, I have no doubt she will be much colder. I will provide her with everything she needs, including my warmth. "Is there anything I can get you?"

"Maybe a little bit of water."

Kala and Evren located a water source during their scouting and brought back several skins full. I pass one to Zara. Once she's had her fill, she gives it back. She makes that tired noise again. "I'm going to try and get some sleep. You'll stay with me?"

"Of course." My heart swells with the knowledge that my mate wants me by her side.

She doesn't say anything, but merely leans her head on my shoulder with an exhausted sigh. Within moments, her breathing has evened out and she emits small snorts. There is nothing that could take me from her now. Not after the trust she shows me.

CHAPTER 9

Zara

There's a hazy mist blocking my view. I squint and scan in front of me from side to side, but it doesn't help. There's nothing but darkness all around me. My heart races and a sense of dread builds in my belly. The kind where I can tell something bad is going to happen. I don't know what and I don't know when, but it's coming. I just have to wait for it. My stomach aches with the nerves, and I do the deep breathing techniques I read about to try and quell the anxiety that is quickly rising. A sharp, stabbing pain hits my chest like I'm having a heart attack.

I keep my breathing slow and even, mentally talking myself down, but nothing I'm doing is helping. The darkness is closing in on all sides. It's like I'm trapped inside a glass cube whose walls grow closer together, pinning me between them. All the air is being sucked out and I can't pull in a breath. My lungs won't inflate, and I'm slowly suffocating. The glass panes move another inch and I'm crouched with my knees pulled to my chest as tightly as I can get them trying to make myself as small as possible. Still, the cube shrinks.

A drop of wetness hits my hand. Then another. And another. I glance down not sure what I'm expecting to find. To my horror, blood drips onto it. I lift my gaze and scream.

"Zara, wake up. It is only a dream. Zara, you must wake." The words are firm, but a gentle touch brushes across my forehead.

My eyes fly open, and I jackknife upright, barely able to catch my breath. Pain engulfs me. My chest aches as I gasp for air. Soft, comforting words are muffled, but slowly become intelligible.

A warm body surrounds me. It should increase the sense of suffocation, but instead I feel safe. Secure. "Breathe, *keeshla*. Slow and easy. It is nothing more than a dream. Be at ease. Breathe. That is it. Breathe again."

My brain finally puts the voice with a face as Kyler continues to whisper encouragement. I don't know how long we sit there with his arms wrapped around me while I mimic his breathing until we're completely in sync. Our chests rise and fall together and with each inhalation we make, my breasts rub across his hard pecs, and arousal stirs in my core. I want to rub myself against him more fully, but the remnants of my nightmare linger. The contradictory emotions play havoc with each other.

Finally, I shift, which Kyler takes as a signal to release me, because his arms loosen and he sits back. We continue touching, but I've lost his embrace. I glance around at camp, but like my horrific dream, I can't see a thing. I strain to listen and can make out the sounds of several different people breathing. If I woke anyone, they don't give any indication.

"Would you like to talk about it?" Kyler asks quietly.

Fuck no. I don't want to relive that shit, but the image will continue to haunt me whether I talk about it or not. I've carried so many burdens for twenty-eight years. It might be nice to share the load with someone.

"I was someplace that was pitch black, and this weird mist surrounded me. It was so real, I could feel the dampness on my skin. I could even smell it, like rain on a spring day." The memory of the clean scent comes back. "But it was like I was locked inside four walls made of glass. With every breath I took, the walls moved closer together until I was forced to sit and try to make myself as small as possible."

A shudder rushes through me as the sensation of them closing in on me returns.

"You are safe, *keeshla.*"

That wasn't even the worst part. Now that I've started talking, I can't stop. "Just when I thought the walls would crush me completely, wet droplets fell on me. I tipped my head back to look up and an eviscerated body was above me dripping blood everywhere."

I turn to face Kyler. "It was me. The body was mine."

That had been the most horrifying part. To see myself covered in blood and my own eyes staring blankly down at me.

Vomit churns in my stomach and I swallow it down.

"Here, drink this." He passes me the skin of water and I take several sips until the queasiness settles.

A harsh breeze kicks up and the cold air nips at my skin. My arm aches, but I do my best to ignore it. I'm not sure I'll be able to go back to sleep. Not after that. But knowing Kyler is here makes me feel better. I've had to rely on myself for more than half my life. Ever since Amelia left. Up until Bryce, I kept everyone at arm's length. Even with him, I never allowed myself to be completely vulnerable.

Watching my friends open themselves up entirely to their mate has been a learning experience. Tavikhi males are nothing like human males. Still, I surprise myself when I ask my question.

"Will you hold me? I don't think I'm going to be able to get back to sleep."

"It would be my honor, *keeshla*," Kyler says.

Taking care with my arm, he lifts me onto his lap and cradles me against his chest. He's so warm and solid beneath me and I rest my head on his shoulder. His sweet eucalyptus scent fills my nose and I breathe it more fully in. Like before, it's a soothing fragrance that eases some of my tension.

I close my eyes and savor it, along with the heat that seeps into me. My muscles relax, and my breathing evens out.

"What made you decide to become a healer?"

"My nene became gravely ill when I was a kit. We all expected her and my baba to travel to the lands of the goddess," he says. "I approached the healer and asked to apprentice with him, because I wanted to learn whatever I could to try and help Nene. He taught me everything he knew, and together we nursed her back to health. When he passed on, I took over as the village healer."

"That must have been scary for a young boy. Watching his mom get sick like that."

Although I can't see it, I get the distinct impression he nods. "It was probably the first time in my life I had been truly terrified. But it was my nene who helped me see that death is nothing to be feared."

I'm not sure I'd go that far, but I'm not one to shit on someone else's beliefs. "I'm glad you were able to save her so you had more time with her and your dad. I take it you all were close? Your brother, too? What was his name?"

"Syler. I believe most Tavikhi families are extremely close, and ours was no exception. Even more so as fewer matings and births occurred," Kyler points out. "Perhaps because we knew that we could soon see the end of our people."

"You all don't have to worry about the end of your people with us humans now, do you? Of course, one of us has to get pregnant first." The minute I give voice to the idea, thoughts of just how to make a baby pop into my head and I'm acutely aware of where I'm sitting.

Kyler must also be distinctly aware, because he shifts beneath me as though suddenly uncomfortable. He clears his throat. "Yes, that does have to happen first."

From what the girls have said, the Tavikhi warriors are virgins, since they don't have casual affairs. As for me, there hasn't been anyone since Bryce. Of course, after what he did there wasn't a chance in hell I was trusting another guy. There also hadn't been many opportunities for any action—even if I'd wanted to—since I left Earth for Tavikh less than two months after all the shit went down. I'd spent the whole time just trying to survive until the ship arrived.

I'm cursing the shit brain Njeri for not only kidnapping me, but for breaking my arm because as much as I'm feeling a little frisky, I'm not in any condition to do so. Certainly not with an audience. My body has other plans anyway. I groan in annoyance.

"I'm going to need some help again." Might as well get over the embarrassment now. "Please."

Like the last time, Kyler helps me to my feet and since I can't see two feet in front of me, he carefully guides me deeper into the forest. I don't bother trying to undo my pants. Instead, I let him take care of it. Thankfully, I've regained enough of my strength I'm able to stand on my own from my squatting position once I'm done. He pulls my pants back up, and together we make our way back to camp.

Kyler pours water on his hands and my uninjured one, which will have to be enough, since we don't have any of the berries that serve as soap.

"Come, let us try and get some more rest before the sun rises. We have a long day of travel ahead of us."

As much as I'm not really tired, he's right. I'm already a liability. The more sleep I get, hopefully the more strength I recover. I've held us up enough. I nod and take his hand so he can guide us back to the spot we vacated a few minutes ago. I hold onto him for support while I lower myself to the ground. Kyler doesn't let me lean up against the tree though. Instead, he situates himself behind me and carefully tugs me so I'm lying against his chest. It's like I have my own personal lounger.

"Remember, you are safe. Nothing can hurt you again," he murmurs in my ear.

I force myself to fully relax into his light embrace. My eyes close and I try to push all thoughts out of my brain and only focus on his words. It isn't long before I feel the pull of sleep. I don't fight it, but rather, let it take me under.

My pallet has never felt this comfortable before. No matter how many furs I stack on it, there's always a lump some-where beneath me. My tent doesn't smell like eucalyptus either. It has the distinct scent of the fire pit. The thing doesn't have to be burning for the smell to fill the air. It's always just…there. This scent is different. It's soothing and makes me want to snuggle farther into the bed. Which I do.

Except the movement brings a whole new awareness. One of pain, and one of a distinct hardness against my lower back. It's then that everything comes back to me. The kidnapping. My broken arm. Kyler's mating marks. The nightmare. Falling asleep against him. Slowly, I open one eye, then the other. Occasional beams of light filter through the trees and everyone is breaking up camp.

My brain registers what exactly is pressing against me, and I manage to sit upright and twist to look at Kyler behind me. A pained expression flits across his face before he quickly erases it. Against my will, I glance down. An impressive bulge is outlined by his leather pants. I squeeze my thighs together, because now isn't the time. It doesn't help. I jerk my gaze away and meet his. Pupils have darkened color and are dilated. At least I'm not the only one affected.

"Good morning."

"Good morning," Kyler's greeting comes out on a husky rasp. "Did you sleep well?"

I guess we're ignoring the charge between us. "I did. Did you?"

"Not in the slightest."

My eyes widen at the admission. "Oh. Sorry."

"It was exquisite torture having you in my arms all night," he continues. "Holding you. Smelling you. Yet not being able to do all the things I have dreamed of doing to you.

Every time I closed my eyes all I could picture was you turning in my arms and kissing me and then lying beneath me so I could pleasure you."

Every drop of saliva in my mouth dries up. What the fuck happened to Kyler? This isn't the same guy from yesterday. The one who lacked confidence and approached me with uncertainty. This is someone new. My tongue flicks out to try and wet my lips. His heated gaze drops to it and for a second, I imagine him claiming my mouth in a fierce kiss. Except he doesn't, and I nearly groan in disappointment.

He blinks and the heat in his gaze disappears. In seconds, he's on his feet and reaches down to help me up. Trying to convince myself that the last two minutes weren't a dream, I clasp his hand and stand. He pours more of that nasty shit powder into a water skin and passes it to me. I drink without him having to tell me. By the time I'm finished, everyone appears ready to head out.

Remi walks over and passes me some meat. "You good to go?"

I'm going to have to be. I've already put us so far behind. "I'm good."

She nods, casts a quick glance in Kyler's direction, and then she returns to Zydon's side. I take a deep breath and start moving.

Kyler will be right next to me the whole time.

CHAPTER 10

KYLER

I have not taken my eyes off Zara the whole day. She has held up surprisingly well, but I sense her increasing fatigue. There have been a few times where she has stumbled, but I have been at her side for each of them to help her recover, which she managed quickly. We have only stopped twice to replenish our water supply and for everyone to take care of their personal needs.

Remi assisted Zara once, but the other time I did. My mate has appeared to get over her embarrassment of asking for my help. While I have tried to treat her as I would one of the injured warriors who comes to see me, I admit to being curious about the human female's body. Not just any female's but Zara's. I caught a glimpse of her bare cunt each time I pulled her leg coverings up. It fascinated me and also made me uncomfortably hard.

"We will rest soon." I will call for it if I have to.

She huffs and braces her free hand on her thigh as she trudges up the hill. I suspect by the time we stop we will have reached the peak, and tomorrow will begin our downward trek to the village.

"Thank God. I'm really trying here, but I swear the oxygen is half of what it normally is and I'm out here sucking wind."

"You have done well, *keeshla*. I know the journey has been difficult, but if we are lucky, then by the next turn of the sun, we will be back in our village." If we are lucky. There still has been no sign of Njeri and only a few sounds of predators within the forest.

"I'm not sure I believe in luck. At least for me." Zara loosens a small laugh. "Now I probably just jinxed it."

"Jinxed?" This is not a word I have heard any humans use.

"It basically means I just screwed us." She glances over and waves her hand in my direction. "Sorry, that didn't help. Um, how to explain jinxed? It's sort of a superstitious thing. It's like me saying 'I've never broken a bone' and then the next day, I break a bone. It's as if I brought it on myself by putting it out there in the universe. It's sort of like calling in bad luck."

I nod. "We do not have a word for this, but I understand what you mean. Let us hope then, that you have not 'jinxed' us."

Although it was not my intent, Zara laughs again, and it is the sweetest sound. "Fingers crossed."

My brow bones shift downward at this new Earth saying. What do crossed fingers have to do with anything?

"You're getting the full human language experience and education today, aren't you?" Zara asks, clearly sensing my continued confusion. "Fingers crossed is sort of the opposite of jinxed. It's like trying to call in good luck."

"Thank you for sharing your language with me. I am intrigued by your various words and manner of speaking." I want to learn everything there is to know about my mate.

I sense the difficulty she has talking and breathing at the same time, so I let the conversation lapse until we rest. Just as I feel Zara has reached her limit, Zydon raises an arm and calls a halt.

"We will make camp here for the night."

"Thank God," my mate gasps out as she bends partway at the waist, supporting her broken arm with the other while she struggles for breath. "I think I've done enough cardio today to last me a lifetime."

"You have done well."

Zara turns her head toward me with a small smile and she slowly stands upright. "Thanks. I don't want to be a burden on anyone."

"You could never be a burden."

Her expression falls and she no longer meets my eyes. "I'm not sure that's true."

I study my mate. Someone has hurt her. Did someone from her past make her feel like a burden? Anger fills my blood with heat. If I ever meet the one who made Zara feel anything but worthy, I cannot promise not to harm them. She deserves to know her worth, and to me, she is nothing but a blessing.

"Come, let us find a spot to rest and ease ourselves." She lets me guide her to a flat area of the forest where several large rocks lie in a formation.

Zara sits against one of them and breathes out a sigh. She swipes her damp brow with the back of her hand. I pass her the skin filled with burim root-infused water. She drinks without prompting.

"I'll never get used to the taste of that stuff, but I suppose after a while it doesn't pack quite the shitty punch as it does the first time." She wrinkles her adorable nose and gives me back the skin.

"It is an acquired taste."

"Well, let's hope this is the last time I ever have to acquire it." Zara makes a sound of distaste that makes me chuckle.

"Fingers crossed."

A laugh explodes from her. "Look at you."

"I am learning your human phrases."

"Nice one."

I dip my head. "Thank you."

We both turn at the sound of someone approaching. Remi draws near and comes to a stop before us. She squats next to Zara.

"How you feeling? You pushed yourself hard today."

My mate blows out a harsh breath. "My legs feel like limp dick and my arm aches like a motherfucker, but other than that, I'm super swell."

Remi's laughter fills the air. "Sounds about right. Luckily, we should be home tomorrow night, if everything goes well."

"That's a big if. There's still a lot of time and space between now and when we reach the village," Zara points out.

"Jesus, pessimist Patty." Remi bumps shoulders with my mate. "I know who not to come to for a pep talk."

"If you wanted rainbow-shitting unicorns, you should have brought Maeve."

My gaze bounces between the two of them, trying to decipher the human phrases they use, but only half of what they are saying makes any sense. One thing I am noticing is that Zara has an unusual fascination with excrement.

"Yeah, she's a much better cheerleader than you. Although, under normal circumstances, you're not too terrible." Remi nudges her again and then slaps her hands on her thighs. "Since you appear to be in good hands, I'm going to head back to my mate. Holler if you need anything."

"Thanks, babe."

Remi gets to her feet and with a final nod in my direction she makes her way back over to Zydon.

"You should eat something." I bring out the cloth-wrapped dreri meat and give the leanest portions to Zara.

Together, we finish off the rest of it.

Once we are done, I bring us water to wash our hands. "Tomorrow should be easier. It is a downhill trek until we reach the village."

"At least that's something in our favor. This is more exercise than I've had in my entire life. I'm not meant for hiking and outdoors." Zara shakes her head. "I'm an upper tier woman through and through."

"What is upper tier?" This is more knowledge I want to soak up about my mate. With every piece I receive it helps me to understand her a little better.

She blows a piece of hair out of her eyes, but it only flops back down so she swipes it away. "It's probably easier to explain if I start back a couple hundred years ago."

I nod for her to continue.

"Back on Earth, the whole place was overpopulated. Separated villages grew outward and melded with other villages until there was practically no land left. All you could see for miles and miles was building after building.

Dwelling after dwelling. They—humans—destroyed all the grasslands and wiped out entire forests. With all the land now covered in buildings, there was no place else to expand villages except up. But building up took credits. Lots and lots of credits," Zara emphasizes. "So, humans were divided into those who had enough credits—upper tier—and those who didn't—bottom tier."

"And you were one of those with lots of credits?"

"Yes," she admits. "Although, technically my dad has all the credits, but obviously, I reaped the benefits."

I try to picture a world where dwellings spread out so far in every direction that they would need to be built on top of each other. It is not an image I can create. "How tall were the dwellings in your upper tier?"

Zara glances around us. "We're about at the top of the mountain range that sits behind the village, right?"

"Yes."

"Taller than that."

My eyes widen. This is where she has come from? A place that does not have bari or trees, but only dwellings that nearly touch the sky as far as one can see?

"If you are this upper tier person with many credits, what was it that brought you to Tavikh?" She spoke of her baba and yet she arrived with the shefira and her other tribe sisters. Why would she leave her family and travel to another planet that is nothing like Earth?

Zara's expression closes off. I have studied her for all these lunar cycles and thought I have seen every emotion, but not this one. Her face is devoid—blank—of all of them. As much as I would like to, I do not push. I want her to trust me with everything, including all her feelings. Her past. Her future. That is what a mating should be like.

"There was nothing left for me back there," she finally says, after far too long of a pause.

I take her hand, because I need her to know that I care. "I may not have any credits, but I will always be here for you no matter what."

Zara smiles, but it is not one of the true ones I have witnessed. This one feels forced, as though she thinks I must see it.

"Thank you." She loosens her hand from mine. "I think I'm going to try and get some sleep. It's still going to be a long day tomorrow."

I stifle my disappointment that she is choosing to push me away. It is as though last night, when she let me hold her in my arms, was only something I made up in my head. Someone has hurt my mate in the past. Was it the baba she spoke of? What about her nene? I dig deep into my well of patience. It will take time for Zara to believe I speak the truth. I must use my actions to prove myself, because when someone has been hurt, words are often not enough.

Soon, she is asleep against the rock, her head at an awkward angle. At the risk of waking her, I sit beside her and gently draw her into my side so she now rests against me. Everyone also settles in for the night, despite the small amount of fading light that manages to creep through the trees. But today was a long day and tomorrow will be equally as long. We will need all the rest we can manage. I glance down at the top of Zara's bari-colored head. I am not sure how much sleep I will get, though.

CHAPTER 11

A lovely smell creeps into my subconscious and I breathe it in again trying to determine exactly what it is. My hip and shoulder are sore from lying on something hard, my legs hurt, and my arm throbs. Hell, my whole body aches. Half of me is cold, while the other half—the side pressed up against a stiff object—is warm and toasty. The object shifts and I become fully alert as the memories of the last few days pour in.

I slowly open my eyes. Leathered lavender skin with black swirling marks greets me. I tip my head back and those bright yellow and purple-black eyes meet mine.

"Good morning. Did you sleep well?" Kyler asks in a sleep-roughened voice.

Considering dried drool is crusted in the corner of my mouth and I don't remember anything since I closed my eyes yesterday, I'd say I slept shockingly rather well. "I did."

"I am glad."

We continue staring at the other, neither of us moving. His warm breath ghosts across my cheek. Are these Tavikhi pure perfection or something? There's not a hint of gross morning breath in the air. Instead, Kyler's smells like he sucked on a mint leaf all night.

I'm sure mine smells like dead and rotting dreri meat. Sometimes life is entirely unfair.

Feeling a bit self-conscious, I blink and break eye contact. Then I carefully push myself upright and adjust my arm that's half out of the sling, wincing at the pain.

"Here."

An animal skin appears in front of me. I take it from him with a mumbled thanks and drink the remainder of the bitter water inside. As nasty as the stuff is, I'll admit it takes the edge off. God knows how much hurt I'd be in if not for the pain reliever.

Now that I'm awake, my bodily functions are making themselves known. "Can I get your help, please?"

"Of course." Kyler brings me to my feet and, like we have several times now, he leads me to a private spot away from everyone and helps me with my pants.

I lost my sense of modesty after that first time. It's pointless. Once I'm finished and wash my hand, we head back to where everyone is once again breaking camp. I'm so ready to get back to the village. The first thing I'm going to do is jump in the river and take a bath. I don't even care how cold it is. I'm absolutely disgusting. I've been ignoring how much I stink and the sweater that's growing over my teeth.

"If we make good time, we should be back to our village before night fall," Zydon announces, his gaze falling to me before quickly skipping away and traveling to the rest of the group.

Message received: don't hold us up, Zara.

Kyler holds something out and I glance down. "We all need our energy."

I take the meat. Everyone has already taken off into the forest so I move as well, eating as I walk. It doesn't take me long to tell that we are, in fact, heading down. It's a huge relief from the upward climb we had yesterday. That sucked. If I never see a mountaintop again it will be too soon.

When we get back to the village, I'm never leaving. Not to welcome any new humans who might arrive by ship to the human settlement that's only about a twenty- or thirty-minute walk from the Tavikhi village. Not to help Sage search for the roots and plants she and Kyler use to make medicine. Nope. I'm keeping my happy ass either at the forge or in my tent. I glance over at the male walking beside me. I suppose now that we're mates, I'll be sleeping in his tent.

Come to think of it, I don't actually know where Kyler's tent is. I mean, there's never been any reason to know. But now I'm curious. In fact, my curiosity encompasses more than just where he lives. I know his parents and brother are dead, but other than that, I don't really know much about him other than he's a great healer who cares about his patients.

"What do you like to do for fun?" Since my lungs aren't dying for air, I can actually talk and breathe at the same time.

"Fun?" Kyler says the word like he doesn't understand its meaning. Damn, maybe he doesn't.

Everything the Tavikhi do is geared toward survival. We've had a few celebrations where we all gather around the central fire and drink, but the occasions have been few and far between.

"Yeah, like when you're not healing people, what do you like to do in your free time that you enjoy? Any hobbies?"

"I enjoy walking through the forest and searching for roots and plants for healing. Is that what you mean by fun?"

Hell no, that's not what I mean. That is the exact *opposite* of what I mean. "Um, what about anything *not* having to do with healing?" Or leaving the village borders.

Kyler pauses for several seconds like he's giving it a lot of thought. Which pretty much tells me everything I need to know. Once again, I'm questioning Deeka. She's given me a guy who is the complete opposite of me. We have nothing in common.

"There is not much else I do," he says cautiously as though knowing that's not at all what I want to hear. "What about you? What do you like to do for…fun?"

It's been a lifetime ago, but when I was little, Amelia and I used to dance. We would find music on our datapads and dance around her room, laughing, and having the best time. I stopped dancing after she died, but there are days I miss it, and lately, I've been finding myself swaying and moving in place when I get dressed in the mornings while I hum a tune…badly.

"Have you ever played Pebbles?"

Kyler's brow bones shift. "I am unfamiliar with that. Is that the stone game the kits play?"

I laugh lightly. "That's the one. I taught Talek, Cecily, and some of the other kids, and now they play each other."

"I have seen this game, but it not something I have experienced for myself."

"I'll have to teach you how to play it when we get back."

My breath catches when two dimples appear on either side of Kyler's curled mouth instead of one. Did I say I'm a sucker for a guy with dimples?

"I would very much enjoy that," he says.

"Me too."

After that, the day progresses and as though we all know we're getting closer and closer to home, our pace picks up slightly. I somehow manage to not slow us down. We stop once for food, water, and to pee and then finally, at long last, the light of several fires is visible through the thinning of the trees. I almost cry with relief that we actually made it. In fact, I can feel the tears well.

"The village knows we are coming by now," Kyler tells me. "The scouts would have let Zander know. I am sure your tribe sisters will be waiting for us to arrive."

Knowing my friends will be waiting makes the tears fall. The only person in my life I knew was a true friend had been Amelia. Until I met London, Remi, Maeve, Sage, and Eloise, that is. Those five women have taught me what genuine friendship is supposed to be. Each and every one of them is like having another sister. I can't always express how much I love them, but I do. More than they'll ever know.

We finally break through the trees to level land near the area of the village where all the elders live. Their central fire burns brightly, and surrounding it appears to be the entire tribe. So many people—Tavikhi and human—stand around and several of them break away and move forward.

The tiniest body rushes toward me. "Zara."

A sob catches in my throat when three more people follow quickly behind her until before I know it, I'm engulfed in the biggest group hug by all my friends. Maeve is bawling and even London, Sage, and Eloise are wiping away tears. Including mine. My arm hurts like a motherfucker, but I don't care. This right here is worth the pain.

"Careful guys. Zara's hurt," Remi lightly scolds them.

"It's…o—okay," I stutter through the tears, not quite ready for them to let go. "I'm okay."

Still, they release their hold but stay closely circled around me.

"We've been so worried about you," Maeve manages through her sobs.

"I was worried about you guys, too. I'm so glad you all are safe." My gaze travels beyond them to the crowd of people and the village behind them.

Despite the sinking sun, it's obvious how much the village has changed while I was gone. There's definitely a fewer number of tents than there were before I was taken. I remember seeing so many of them on fire and all the smoke that day. My heart aches for everything we've lost.

"Holy shit." London gapes at something behind me.

Everyone's gaze shifts in that direction and several people suck in breaths. The hairs on the back of my neck stand up and I can literally feel the heat of a warm body as someone stands close. I don't have to look to know it's Kyler, and yet, I turn my head and meet his eyes over my shoulder. Just knowing he's here helps calm me for some reason. I face my friends again.

"I guess some good came out of me getting abducted."

London laughs. "Only you could get kidnapped and come back mated."

"What can I say? I like to keep things interesting." I grin widely.

Someone approaches, and I glance in that direction to find Zander joining our group. He stands next to London and wraps his tail around her. It hits me that the only time Kyler has done the same is when he's stopped me from falling on my face. Will he, too, one day wrap it around me as a sign of affection?

Then, to my surprise, Zander takes a step forward, reaches for my free hand, and presses his brow bones to it. "We are so happy to have you home, sister. You have been greatly missed. And blessings on your mating."

Goddamn it. The tears that just dried up flow again. He releases me and returns to London.

"Thank you Shefir, but Zara needs to rest," Kyler's voice comes from almost right next to my ear.

A warm hand settles on my back, and I want nothing more than to lean my weight against him. Wait, why shouldn't I? He's my mate, right? Fuck it. I move into his space and press myself to his side. I wanted a bath, but now that we're here, all I want to do is sleep for days.

"Go. Take all the time you need to heal," Zander says.

Being careful with my arm this time, the girls each give me one last hug before everyone disperses.

"Come, *keeshla*."

I let Kyler guide me through the village. It isn't until we're standing outside my tent that I realize where we are. I glance at him in surprise. He must sense my confusion.

"As much as I would like for you to join me in my tent, I am sure you would prefer being in your own furs for the time being," he says by way of explanation. "We have the rest of our lives for you to sleep in my furs."

I'm slightly irritated that Kyler just assumed this is where I wanted to be without even asking me. I had enough of other people making decisions for me back on Earth to last me a lifetime. Except I'm too tired to argue with him tonight. He pushes aside the flap. I step inside and nearly sob in relief that someone has lit a torch and planted it near the fire pit to give me some light to see.

Everything is exactly how I left it—messy furs, clothes tossed everywhere—which means that I was one of the lucky ones whose stuff wasn't torched by the Njeri. I almost feel guilty over the fact, but then I was kidnapped, so maybe it's a fair trade.

"Get some sleep, *keeshla*," Kyler says, interrupting my thoughts. "I will see you in the morning."

He takes a step back and the flap drops.

"Wait." I move quickly forward to stop it, but he's already there holding it open again. I worry my bottom lip and fidget with the hem of my shirt. "Will you…will you stay? Please?"

Kyler blinks his feline eyes. My anxiety spikes and I open my mouth to tell him to forget it.

"You honor me with your trust, *keeshla*," he says. "Will you be all right for a few moments while I check on the injured warriors? I promise I will return as quickly as I can."

Of course he would want to look in on those who'd been wounded during the battle.

I nod. "I'll be fine."

Kyler hesitates for a second, and the next thing I know, he's inside my tent with my head cradled between his palms and kissing me. It's quick and hard, but I feel it all the way to my toes. He ends the kiss and rests his brow bones gently against my forehead. Both of us are breathing hard.

"I *will* return."

"Okay," I whisper.

As suddenly as he closed the distance between us, Kyler's gone. The torch flame flickers from the breeze created by the flap closing over the entrance. I stand there for the longest time before finally taking a seat on my furs to wait for him to come back.

CHAPTER 12

KYLER

My pace quickens as I hurry to the healer's tent to check on the wounded. Lit torches stand outside the entrance, and I push aside the flap guarding it. When I had left, seven warriors and humans occupied beds within. A quick glance confirms that two beds are now empty.

Sage and Jodah stand near the supply table speaking quietly with each other, but they look over at my arrival. My apprentice approaches with a smile and clasps my hands.

"I knew you guys would find Zara," she says after a reassuring squeeze and releases her hold on me. "Although you coming back as her mate is something of a shock."

"It was a surprise to me as well."

Jodah joins us and fists his chest. "Blessings on your mating."

"Thank you." I return the gesture and shift my gaze to the vacant furs. "Did our tribe brothers travel to the lands of Deeka?"

Sage's expression falls and sorrow crosses her face. "I—*we*—did everything we could."

I lay my hand on her shoulder. "Of that I have no doubt. You are a wonderful healer."

She smiles sadly and nods. "Thank you. The rest are still hanging on. They've all woken up and spoken at least once but are still in pain. London and Jodah have been out in the forest replenishing our supplies daily. Unless something drastic happens, I suspect the remaining wounded will make a full recovery."

It would appear she and her mate have things well in hand. "I will return first thing in the morning. In the meantime, I must get back to Zara's tent."

"Go," she urges. "Everyone is stable. If I need you for something, I'll send Jodah."

With a final glance at the sleeping warriors, I exit and quickly make my way back to my mate. Now that we have returned, the village has quieted. People have entered their tents while several warriors and human males appear to be maintaining guard and patrolling. It is clear Zander is taking extra precautions. The Njeri attack had blindsided us. I assume the Krijese traveled back to their village within the hills. My sole attention had been on getting Zara safely to her dwelling to rest.

I reach her tent and slap the door flap. In only a few beats of my heart, it swings open, as though my mate had been standing close by in anticipation of my arrival. She shifts to the side and I step past her and into her dwelling. I sweep my gaze around and take it fully in. When I brought her here earlier, my focus had only been on her, but looking around, I am able to learn a few things about my mate. The primary thing is that she is messy. I turn back toward her. She remains by the entrance, her eyes darting everywhere but on me.

"If you have changed your mind about wanting me to stay, you only have to let me know," I rush to reassure her. "I will not be upset."

Zara rattles her head. "No, it's not that. Sage has told me how meticulous and orderly you are with your medical supplies. I'm going to bet that means your tent is the same. I'm just realizing how chaotic mine probably feels to you and that I should have picked up a little before you came back. I'm sure you think I'm a slob."

Carefully, I close the distance between us, making sure to step over her pallet of furs and not on it. I cradle her cheek and a rumble of satisfaction nearly bursts from my chest when Zara leans into my touch. "Perhaps a little chaos is not such a bad thing. Maybe this is why Deeka chose us as mates. She knew that we would bring out the best in each other and encourage us to be more accepting of our differences. I believe we are the perfect complement to one another."

Wetness gleams in my *keeshla's* eyes. "If you're trying to get me to fall in love with you, I'd say you're doing a damn good job of it so far."

My heart nearly bursts with joy. Everything I have dreamed of since I was a kit is coming to me. I lean in and pause just before my lips touch Zara's. "Then I must keep trying until you have completely fallen."

With that, I claim her mouth with mine. I thread my hand through her hair and tilt her head to deepen our connection. A flicker of something against my lips has me drawing away and staring down at her. Is this a new form of kissing?

"Sorry, did that gross you out or something?" she asks.

"Not at all. I was only unsure of what it was. Is this a different style of kissing?"

Zara swallows and nods. "It's considered more intimate when partners kiss with their tongues."

Kissing with tongues? "I would like to try this more intimate kiss with you again. Please."

This time it is she who initiates. She rises up on her toes and presses her lips to mine. It starts out as the few other kisses we have shared, but then there is that flick of a touch again. I part my mouth, and she sweeps fully inside, engaging my tongue with tentative swipes as though testing out my flavor. It is the most divine sensation I have ever experienced. Wanting more, I move closer and pull Zara against me.

She cries out and breaks the kiss. I release her in an instant and curse myself for causing her pain. She cradles her arm more tightly to her chest.

"Apologies, *keeshla*. I never meant to hurt you. Please forgive me."

"It's okay," she says in a soothing tone. "We both got a little carried away."

I jerk my chin in her direction. "May I?"

Zara nods.

Taking great care, I examine her arm. "I need to adjust the splint. It has come loose."

She grimaces, but braces herself. "Can you do it standing or would it be easier if we're sitting?"

Sitting would be best, but I will let her decide. "Whichever you are most comfortable with."

"Then my answer is neither." Zara chuckles but releases a sigh. "Let's just get it over with. I'll try not to whine too much."

She moves to her pallet and settles onto it with her legs crossed. I take my place directly in front of her and mimic her pose. She slips her arm out of the support and I gently take it in my hands. Working as swiftly as I can and doing my best to make the process as painless as possible, I adjust the sticks that comprise the splint and tighten their bindings.

Zara flinches a few times, but otherwise doesn't move until I finish and replace the length of cloth cradling her injured limb. She raises it up and down before setting it back in her lap. "It actually does feel better now. Thank you."

"You are most welcome." It is my honor to serve her. "Do you need anything more for the pain?"

She shakes her head. "I'm good. I don't want to rely too heavily on it. Besides, it's not going to kill me to have an ache or two here and there."

"Or perhaps, I suspect, it is because you are tired of drinking shit."

Laughter explodes from Zara. "I think I'm a bad influence on you. I'm not sure I have ever heard a Tavikhi curse."

"We do, but it most likely does not translate into your Earth language. Although, I understand the shefir has adopted one of the human's curses. Fuck, I believe it is?" It is not a word I have ever spoken until now, but hearing it come from my tongue, I can understand why Zander might like it.

"Oh man," Zara says with evident amusement. "You can't go wrong with fuck as a curse. It's one of my favorites. Teach me one of your curse words, will you?"

I pause for a moment while I consider one she might like. "There is budalla. Or what about dhise?"

She smiles and it is so bright it is as though the light of an entire sky full of suns shines down. "I really like budalla. What does it mean?"

"In your language it would closely translate to the cock of a dhibani."

"Oh my God, that is absolutely perfect. I'm going to start using that." Zara cackles like a burracak. "Man, Clifton and Priscilla would shit over that one. I can see Priscilla's lips pinched in disdain already. And Clifton looking down his stuck-up nose."

I tilt my head. These are not names I know. She glances at me and must read the confusion on my face.

"Sorry. Clifton and Priscilla are my parents. A couple of tight-asses. Which, by the way"—she holds up a finger—"is not a good thing. They're both snobs of the highest order. Thinking they're better than everyone, including me."

The memory of her speaking of her baba having many credits returns to me. What else did she say about him? Or her nene? "You did not have a good relationship with your baba and nene, then?"

Zara makes a harsh noise. "They were some of the worst parents a person could have. To be perfectly honest," she pauses and takes a deep breath. Her eyes meet mine. "I hated them. Which to some people might make me a terrible daughter, but I don't care."

I reach for her hand and hold it gently between mine, caressing it with a finger. "I think you must have a very good reason to feel as you do. If you are in any way worried I am one of those people who believes you to be terrible, then you should not be. I do not think there is anything you could do that would make me think you are terrible."

Wetness gleams in Zara's eyes. "You really need to stop being so damn nice."

There is no harshness in her words so I do not truly believe she means them. I reach up and swipe away a stray tear that glides down her cheek. A smile creeps onto my face. "I will do my best to be less nice."

"No you won't," she says.

No, I will not. A voice tells me that not many people have been kind to my mate, which means I will need to shower Zara with every bit of kindness that I can. She deserves it. "We should get some rest."

She nods. "You're probably right. Although I better take care of my personal business first."

I help her up, and together, we leave for the area where we take care of our needs. In no time, we are back at her tent and cleaned up. I watch as she uses a special paste and cleanses her teeth with a bristled device of some kind.

"I've never been so glad to be able to brush my teeth as I am now," Zara says when finished. "I don't know how you can stand talking to or kissing me with my breath smelling as awful as it did."

"Nothing about you smells bad." Beneath the dirt, there is only the scent of female.

She shudders and carefully lowers herself onto her furs. "Then your nose doesn't work. As soon as I get up tomorrow, I'm taking a bath in the river. You may not be able to smell my stench, but I can. After that, I'm burning these clothes."

I hesitate, because although Zara has asked me to stay, I do not want to presume that also means she wants me to sleep beside her as we did out in the forest. Once she has laid down and made herself comfortable, she glances up.

"You're not going to just stand there all night are you?"

"If you ask me to I will." There is nothing I would not do for her.

She pats the ground next to her. "I'm not asking you to."

I slip my sheathed sword over my head and lay it on the ground beside the fire pit. Next, I remove the satchels from around my waist and place them beside the weapon, until I am clad in only my leg coverings. They are not something I normally wear during sleep, but I do not believe Zara is ready for me to remove them. She remains wearing the same leg and chest coverings she had on when she was taken.

At last, I lay down at her side. She moves close, curls up against me, and rests her injured arm over my chest. I have never been more content in all of my life. Emotion swells within my heart. At long last, Deeka has blessed me with a mate. There is no more joyous moment than this one.

"Thank you for staying." Her breath caresses my flesh and my mating marks tingle where it blows across them. I can sense them darkening in the pale light.

"It is my pleasure." One of these turns, my *keeshla* will understand there is nothing that I would not do for her. I kiss the top of her head. "Rest, Zara."

She mumbles and nods. I lie there long after her breathing evens out, listening to the soft sounds and noises she makes, until finally I let myself relax enough that I join her in sleep.

CHAPTER 13

ZARA

The same familiar scent I've woken up to for the last three days invades my senses, and I smile against the warm body I'm practically lying on top of. Despite the lingering aches everywhere, I'm not entirely uncomfortable. The ground beneath me is much softer than it's been now that I'm sleeping in my furs in my own tent, even with the familiar lump I've grown used to. Something I can finally admit I wasn't entirely positive would ever happen.

While I was with the Njeri, I refused to even think about the possibility I wouldn't make it back to the Tavikhi village, but deep down, where I'd buried every negative outcome, the knowledge that there was a chance I'd die was present. It almost feels like this is just a dream and when I wake up, I'll be back with those fuck faces.

I breathe in Kyler's comforting scent and slowly open my eyes so I can ground myself in the here and now. That sense of relief hits at the sight of lavender skin and black mating marks. Light filters in through the opening above and shines directly on his face. His eyes remain closed, and I take the time to study his features.

There are a few more noticeable fine lines around his eyes and between his brow bones. He has more white strands of hair than yellow ones and there are a few patches here and there across his shoulders and along his chest where his skin shade is slightly paler than the rest. To the point I'd even consider it gray. Kyler's still sexy as fuck. I'm not sure how I got this lucky, but I'm not going to question it again.

I shift closer, almost rubbing against him like a cat in heat —completely forgetting about my injury—until pain shoots through me, and I hiss. His eyes open and he's instantly alert.

"What is wrong? Where are you hurt?"

My cheeks heat with embarrassment over trying to dry hump him and I wave him off. "I'm fine. This damn arm keeps getting in my way."

Kyler studies me for a second and I can almost swear he knows exactly what I'd been doing. I try not to flinch under his steady gaze. Finally, he blinks, and the connection is broken. He sits up and I brush off the fact my feelings are a little hurt that he didn't even try to kiss me good morning. Maybe he was just being nice when he said my breath didn't stink. I brushed my teeth last night, but that doesn't mean the freshness hasn't worn off.

He turns slightly and stares down at me. "Are you hungry? I will bring us something to eat before I must go back to the healer's tent to check in on the wounded again."

"I'm okay. You go ahead." I push myself upright. "I'm going to go find one of the girls to help me with a bath. I'm so ready to feel clean again."

"You will be careful?" Kyler asks.

I nod. "Of course."

He hesitates for only a second, and as though sensing my disappointment, he leans forward and kisses me. It's brief, but no less powerful than any others we've shared. Except I want more. I thought I'd get it last night, but then this stupid broken arm had to go and cock-block me. Kyler draws away and gets to his feet.

"I will see you at the midday meal?"

That long? *Jesus, when did I become such a needy bitch*? "Yes, I'll see you then."

His eyes stay locked on mine for a minute until finally, he dips his head and walks out. I stare at the flap, waiting for him to come back, but it remains closed. With a heavy sigh, I flop back onto my furs and sling my good forearm over my eyes.

I'm not sure how long I lay there, but there's a slapping sound against the door flap. "It's Eloise. Can I come in?"

"Yeah."

I move my arm to expose one eye and squint at the light that shines in through the entrance as she steps inside.

"You okay down there?" she chuckles.

"I'm wasting away from the lack of dick." I slowly push myself to sitting again and huff in annoyance. "Why can't these Tavikhi males be a little less gentlemanly?"

"Because they love and respect their women and sometimes tend to be a little over-protective."

Eloise and I share a look before bursting out laughing.

"Okay, so maybe a lot over-protective," she clarifies. "But that's what makes them such amazing guys. They'll do anything for us. Especially when they think we might get hurt. It's in their DNA to care for their mates."

"I know. This stupid broken arm isn't doing me any favors though." I raise it. "How long do bones take to heal, anyway?"

She winces. "Usually around eight to twelve weeks."

"Two or three months?" I croak out. "Are you telling me that Kyler isn't going to do more than kiss me for the next two or three months?"

"I mean, I'm sure there are things you could do to persuade him otherwise." She shrugs. "It's not as though you don't have any feminine wiles. Use them."

This is why I like Eloise. She isn't above doing what needs to be done to get what she wants. From hearing her tell it, she's the one who seduced Zedam. I'm not above seducing Kyler. I just wish this stupid splint and sling weren't in the way. It's hard to be sexy when I've got this thing strapped across my chest.

"You're right. I have wiles. They might be a little rusty, but I definitely have them." At least, I think I do. "Let's start with getting my stank-ass clean. Because I do not feel sexy in any way smelling like socks that have been soaked in sweat and piss for ten days and then set out in the desert heat to cook the scent in."

Eloise makes a gagging sound. "That is not the visual I needed."

She holds out a hand, and with her help, I climb to my feet. "Let me grab some clean clothes and soap."

I rifle through everything in the pile I know is actually clean and manage to snag what I need, although I have to sniff the jeans to make sure they aren't really dirty. Eloise helps me carry some of it. As we leave my tent, I get my first good glimpse of the village in the daylight.

"So much was destroyed." My eyes burn seeing the destruction as I take it all in while we walk toward the river.

"It was, but we're rebuilding," Eloise says. "Even some of the humans from the settlement have been here to help."

"Really?" I know relations between the Tavikhi and the humans that opted to stay back in the settlement after the Krijese attack that brought London, me, and the rest of my friends here have improved slightly over the last nearly five months, I just hadn't realized they'd improved *that* much.

"I think Gary and Adam finally accepted the fact that things would be better for them if they were on good terms with the people who could actually protect them if the Njeri decide to invade them," Eloise points out. "Look what happened here with a village full of trained warriors. The humans at the settlement wouldn't stand a chance. Although, if I'm being honest, I'm kind of surprised they didn't start there, all things considered."

We reach the riverbank and come to a stop.

"Everybody there is lucky. The only reason I can think they started here was because it *was* harder. I mean, if they could take out the Tavikhi warriors, then raiding the human settlement after that would be a cake walk." It's the only thing that makes sense. "Handicap our village so we have to use all our resources to protect ourselves and then go for the weak ones."

Eloise nods. "You might be right. I just hope that doesn't mean the Njeri are regrouping and planning to try again."

"Let's hope." I sigh and then grin. "Well, I guess you're the lucky one who gets to help me get naked."

She laughs. "Yay, me."

"Didn't think this all the way through when I mentioned needing a bath, did you?" I hold up my broken arm.

"I did not, but don't say I'm not a good friend who helps someone out in need." Eloise walks over and together we somehow manage to get me out of my clothes.

She hands me the berries we use as soap, and I pad out into the water. "Motherfucker, it's cold."

"Don't be such a baby," she calls out.

I give her the finger as I wade farther into the deeper area. All she does is chuckle. Once I'm submerged up to my chest, I quickly wash my entire body as best I can. When I'm done, I do it again until I finally feel human. Now comes the hard part. I hold my broken arm up in the air and dunk my entire body. In seconds, I come up sputtering and swiping hair out of my face.

"Fuuuuuuuck."

"Need some help out there?" Eloise hollers and it's clear she's trying not to laugh.

"I hate you right now."

"You love me," she sing-songs.

With a disgruntled huff, I make my way back to shore. "I can't wash my hair."

"Come on, let's get you dressed, and then you can lie down."

With her help, I manage to get my clean clothes on and positioned on my back so I can tilt my head into the water. Eloise quickly lathers up the soap and threads her fingers through the wet strands. To my surprise, she gives an amazing head massage. I peer up at her.

"You're good at this."

A flash of sadness crosses her face. "I had to help my friend Johnna wash her hair back on our ship after she broke her wrist."

The terraforming ship Eloise worked on had been attacked by space pirates, and she and her friends managed to make it off the thing in escape pods before it exploded. The aftershocks sent the pods in different directions, so she has no idea what happened to her crewmates, or if they're even alive.

I reach up and lay my hand on top of hers. I don't want to offer false words of hope, because we have no way of knowing Johnna's all right. I squeeze Eloise's hand in support. "I pray she was as lucky as you."

She offers me a small smile and finishes washing my hair in silence. Once it's rinsed out, she squeezes as much moisture out of it as she can and helps me to my feet. I manage to get my arm back in the sling with only the slightest bit of help. I'm sure I'm going to have to have Kyler adjust the splint again. It'll be worth it though to feel clean.

We walk back toward the village where there's a ton of commotion. Eloise and I glance at each other before we take off jogging toward the central fire where we can already see tribespeople gathering. But they're not alone. Fear shoots through me and my steps stutter until I realize no alarms are being sounded. In fact, Zander steps forward and clasps arms with a stranger.

An extremely beautiful male stranger wearing a tight-fitting, black sleeveless shirt that accentuates a muscular build to rival most of the Tavikhi and matching pants that mold just a little too well to his…oh wow. I almost choke. His copper skin shimmers in the sunlight and his short, teal hair has the perfectly tousled look as though someone weaved their fingers through it to muss it *just enough*.

I squint. Are those horns peeking through, too?

Oh my God, they are. Well, hello, new mister alien man.

CHAPTER 14

Kyler

Sleeping beside my mate had been another night of agony. I had woken up more than once to find Zara's body nearly draped over mine. My hard cock had made it difficult to return to sleep when I had wanted to do nothing more than wake her with kisses and slide into the warm heat of her cunt. My mating nodes had been preparing for that very thing and leaked the mating fluid all males possess that is meant to enhance our mate's pleasure.

But I must resist. Zara is healing and still recovering from her ordeal. As much as I wish to take her to my furs, I have to control my urges until she is well. Still, thoughts of her bathing have invaded my mind all day, distracting me from my work. I have pictured her bare cunt countless times as well as imagined my hands running over her wet and naked body as I help her wash. My fingers ache to explore her chest mounds, along with the rest of her.

Loud voices from outside the tent draw my attention. I finish smearing the healing salve on Rojtar's chest, which is looking well, and cleanse my hands. When I step outside, the sun is high in the sky, and a pleasant breeze brings with it the scent of burning fiku wood and the faint odor of the nenuphar bushes that are blooming all along the banks of the river. Several warriors carrying sparring staffs stride past in the direction of the central fire. There does not appear to be a sense of urgency, but the memory of the recent Njeri attack is not far from my mind.

"Is all well?"

Katem glances at me. "The Bohnari have arrived."

With everything that has gone on over the last few turns, I had forgotten that our allies from the neighboring planet were going to be landing here soon. We have been trading with their tribe since I was a kit. I follow the warriors to greet our visitors.

Tribespeople have already begun to gather. It is always a celebration when the Bohnari arrive. The elders bring out their special drink, and our people trade stories long into the night. Perhaps this is what Zara meant when she asked about having fun. It is always an enjoyable time when our allies visit.

Zander welcomes Alik, the Bohnari leader, with a fist to his chest as a sign of respect and the two males clasp forearms. A sudden tingling of my mating marks turns my head. As though a tether links us together my eyes land on

Zara. She wears clean coverings and her hair lies wet down her back with several droplets sliding down the side of her face. In her arms are her dirty chest and leg coverings. My heart leaps at the sight of her. Only she is not looking at me. Her gaze is locked on Alik and the obvious interest on her face stabs me straight in the chest. I do not believe she has ever gazed upon me with the same expression.

Eloise nudges my mate in the side and Zara shifts her gaze until it lands on me. She smiles widely and redirects her steps to approach me. The scent of berries drifts on the breeze, but beneath it is my mate's own unique scent.

"Hey, you," she greets me. "I see we have a visitor. This one looks to be a friendly though."

Something twists inside my gut despite her perceived happiness at seeing me. Humans do not feel the bond like Tavikhi do. Just because she is my mate until I travel to the lands of Deeka, it does not mean it is the same for her. There is nothing tying her to me if she chooses someone else.

"Is something wrong?" Zara asks, breaking into my thoughts. "You're looking at me weird."

I force a smile to my mouth. "Apologies. All is well."

She does not appear to believe me but does not question my reply. Instead, she gestures at the Bohnari leader who moves around the fire and greets several of the elders who have approached. "I take it this guy's a friend?"

Before Zara looked at Alik the way she did, I would have said yes, but a vicious emotion blooms inside me, and I have a sudden desire to punish him for daring to arrive at our village now. I force down the urge and manage a nod.

"He is a Bohnari who lives on the neighboring planet. The rest of his warriors will be here soon."

"Oh, yeah, I've heard about them from Benham. They're the ones who provide him with the metal he uses in the forge to make your weapons." Her eyes widen when she once again looks upon Alik. "I've been curious about them since. Aren't they also the ones who gave you all your translators?"

"Yes. We trade with them at the beginning of every warm season."

"Cool. I wonder what other kinds of things they have that we might be able to use?" Zara asks.

There is an intense desire to grab her and run away so she has no chance of speaking with any of the Bohnari males. This is not a feeling I have ever experienced before, this possessive need to let every male know that she is mine. It started on the trip back here with Rassim, even though he is mated. But the Bohnari do not have females on their planet after some great disease ripped through their species and took them all.

"I am not sure." The words are dragged out of me against my will.

It is then that Alik draws nearer to where we stand. I do not want him speaking to Zara.

"How was your bath?" I do my best to distract her.

Far too slowly, she pulls her gaze away from the Bohnari leader to meet my eyes. "It was great. I feel like a new woman. You're probably going to have to tighten my splint again."

That is the perfect excuse to take her away from here. "Come then, let us return to your tent, and I will take care of it."

"Healer," a booming voice echoes.

I turn to find Alik approaching. His gaze moves to Zara and scans her from head to toe. I do not like the look in his eyes, and a feral growl rumbles up from my chest. Both his and my mate's heads jerk in my direction, hers with widened eyes and a gaping mouth. Alik, on the other hand, smirks and my fists clench with the need to strike him across the face.

"It would seem congratulations are in order on your mating," he says. "Your goddess chose a beautiful female."

Zara's cheeks turn a different color, and she dips her head. Needing to show him who she belongs to, I wrap my tail around her waist and drag her against my side. She stumbles slightly and sucks in a breath, but I quickly right her. Thankfully, she remains where she is, but there is a rigid tension to her.

"I'm Zara." She introduces herself after a sharp glare in my direction and stretches out her hand.

The Bohnari leader glances down at it and then places his own within hers. "I have heard of this thing you humans call a handshake. Greetings, Zara. I am Alik."

"Nice to meet you."

He flicks his gaze to mine before meeting hers again. One side of his mouth curls up. He still has not released her. "The pleasure is most certainly mine."

The growl rumbles from my chest again, but Alik is not at all bothered. Zara, on the other hand, grows even more tense. As though sensing I have reached my limit, he lets go of her. He gestures to her injured arm. "Come to our ship later to meet with our healer. He can repair that for you."

With those words, he walks away and greets Zydon and several of the other warriors who have joined the group. The moment he is out of hearing range, Zara shoves her elbow into my side—pushing herself away—and whirls on me.

"What the hell is wrong with you?" she hisses like an angry luani kit. "You were acting like a damn caveman."

"I do not know what a caveman is."

She puffs out her chest mounds and walks stiffly for a few steps with an exaggerated swing of her shoulders. "I'm a big, tough man," she says in a deep voice. "Let me swing my dick around and show you who's got the bigger one."

I have heard this word...dick. I glance down. "My cock is average size, but it is not swinging around. It is inside my leg coverings."

This time it is Zara who growls. "For fuck's sake, it's a figure of speech. Seriously though, what is your problem?"

"I did not like the way Alik was looking at you." The admission is dragged from me.

She gapes. "Are you kidding me?"

My only response is silence. She narrows her eyes and stomps away. I follow. Zara does not stop until she reaches her tent. With a rough yank, she jerks open the flap and goes inside. I only hesitate for a beat before I continue in behind her. She throws down her dirty coverings and spins with a hand on her hip.

"You know, I always thought it would be hot to have a man all jealous and possessive over me, but now I don't think I do. I'm actually pretty annoyed."

Is that what this emotion in that swirls and rages inside me? Jealousy? "You are my mate."

"And that gives you the right to manhandle me? Because some guy was talking to me?" She tosses up her good arm.

"He wanted to do more than talk, and you were looking at him the same way."

Zara flinches and sucks in a harsh breath. Her bottom lip trembles. "Is that the kind of person you think I am? Just because I think a guy's attractive, you think I'm going to spread my legs for him even though I have a husband—a mate?"

Her questions make my entire body go still. I even believe my heart stops beating. A bitter emotion spirals through me.

Shame.

It settles like a massive stone in my belly. I swallow, and my shoulders drop in ugly defeat as I bow my head and stare at the ground. "I am a fool. While I am undeserving of your forgiveness, I will beg for it anyway, and do not blame you if you do not give it. From the depth of my soul, you have my apologies for hurting you, Zara, and for being such an unworthy male to a female who has done nothing to earn my jealousy."

Footsteps approach, but I do not raise my head. I am not fit to even gaze upon my mate's face. If she chooses to reject me, it is my own fault, and I will live with the consequences of my actions. A small, warm hand cradles my cheek.

"Look at me, Kyler," Zara commands softly.

Slowly, I lift my gaze to hers. She does not smile or offer me words of comfort. As well she should not.

"We're both new to this whole mating thing, so we're learning as we go," she strokes my skin gently. "I am *your* mate. But I am also a female. Just because I find another male attractive does not mean that there is anything between us or that there ever will be. It hurt—*a lot*—that you would think I would do something like that. That's not who I am."

"I know."

"Then why?"

Once again shame fills me and I step back, breaking our connection. I cannot look Zara in the eyes as I make a confession. "I was not entirely truthful with you before."

"About what?"

"I was not close to my brother." This is the first time I have spoken the truth to anyone outside of my family.

She moves in front of me and to my surprise, takes my hand and leads me to her pallet. "I feel like we should be sitting for this conversation."

Together, we take a seat on her furs, once again facing each other. Zara does not loosen her hold on my hand and for that I am grateful. She gives me her strength.

"Tell me about Syler."

CHAPTER 15

If anyone else would have said the things to me that Kyler did and made me feel the way he had, I would have kicked them in the balls. But beneath his apology I had felt his deep pain. Something caused him to act like a jealous jerk.

Amelia always said I could hold a grudge better than anyone, but this is my mate. My husband. The person I am going to spend the rest of my life with. Having an open line of communication is important. Even when I'm angry. But mostly, really hurt.

Kyler sighs heavily. "Syler was much younger than me. For the longest time, my nene and baba believed I would be their only kit. Until I was not. As he grew older, it became obvious there was something different about him.

He was always angry. Cruel. To the rest of the tribe, he hid it behind smiles and laughter. He was sly in that way."

I've known those kinds of people. The ones who have a public persona in vast contrast to their private self.

"As I said before, healing became my passion," Kyler continues. "I trained as a warrior because I had to, not because I wanted to. Of all the males in the village, I have always been one of the leanest. I do not have the strength and power the warriors and hunters do. Syler did. In fact, he was one of the strongest males in the village and never let me forget it."

Already I don't like this guy. "He sounds like a giant tool."

Kyler cocks his head. "Is that another human figure of speech?"

I chuckle. "It's a derogatory name for someone. Basically, he sounds like a shithead."

"Ah, yes. Excrement is a proper enough description. Syler *was* a 'shithead'."

I press my lips together, trying not to laugh, because as hilarious as it is to hear Kyler call his brother that, this is a serious conversation that holds a lot of hurts. "Go on."

He pauses a second and glances away before meeting my eyes. "There was a female once."

"A female?" I croak.

"Yes. She was ten warm seasons younger than me, and we became friends. She had an interest in plants and roots. As we grew older, I had great hopes that one day she would be my mate," he says slowly as though softening the blow.

"I see." How I manage to sound normal is beyond me. Suddenly Kyler's possessiveness and jealousy doesn't seem so petty anymore. "What happened? I mean, obviously you two weren't fated mates."

"My brother."

Ouch. "Was she his mate, then?"

He shakes his head. "No, but he knew how I felt about her. Soon, he began spending time with her, especially after I became the village healer. I grew busier and he took advantage of the fact. He would also remind her how much older I was than both of them and that if I hadn't found a mate yet, it must be because Deeka did not find me worthy. It was not long before she looked at him the way I, no doubt, looked at her. As though she wished for nothing more than to be his mate."

What a dick. "He tried to make you jealous."

"That is it," Kyler says, "I was not. I was hurt and angry, but I was not jealous. Not like I was today when you looked at Alik the way Mera looked at Syler."

I wince, because I *had* ogled the Bohnari. He is absolutely gorgeous, and I'm not dead. Of course, that doesn't mean I want to get into a relationship with the dude, but I can see how that makes my mate feel. "I'm sorry. I didn't mean to hurt you or make you feel like I was in any way interested in him, because I'm *not*."

"Humans do not feel the mate bond like Tavikhi do, so I can understand if you might experience a want for another male." Kyler hisses in pain and rubs his side where I'd pinched him as hard as I could. "Why did you do that?"

"Because I don't like the fact you made an assumption that just because I think a guy is hot that I want to have sex with him. I can see an attractive man and not want to fuck him or be his wife, thank you very much. Especially when I already have a mate. Just because I'm human, doesn't mean I'm a disloyal bitch."

Kyler shakes his head. "I do not think you are disloyal."

"Sure could have fooled me. I may not have a soul light, but that doesn't mean I can't feel a bond with someone— with *you*. It's called love, you big jerk."

He blinks rapidly and draws back a fraction. "Are you saying you love me?"

"I'm *saying* I'm pretty sure I'm falling in love with you." That had been easier than I thought it would be. "That's not going to stop because I lay eyes on a good-looking guy or one talks to me. I'm not that shallow. Looks are great and all, but there are far more important traits. Besides, gorgeous guys become ugly if they're terrible people."

Kyler palms my cheek. "No warrior is as lucky as I to have a mate as kind and forgiving as you. I have made many mistakes in my life, but none I have regretted more than hurting you."

I cover his hand with mine. "Just try not to do it again, please. I'm not sure my heart can take it."

"The rest of my seasons will be spent making it up to you."

"You don't have to do that. Just continue being a good mate." I'm not going to hold this over his head for the rest of his life. I'm not that big of an asshole.

Kyler leans in and pauses before brushing his lips across mine. Maybe to make sure I'm going to let him. When I don't stop him, he kisses me softly and sweetly before pulling back enough to meet my eyes. "I will make sure to be the best of mates."

"I'm sure you will." This time, I kiss him.

He slips his tongue between my lips like he's been kissing his entire life, and the mint flavor of his mouth fills mine. *Still totally unfair.* Kyler deepens the kiss and all thoughts of fairness disappear to be replaced with pleasure and need and want. The urge to take my mate to bed rises up full force.

Eloise's words come back to me. *Use your feminine wiles.* Right, I'm supposed to have those. Being extra cautious so I don't bump myself, I slowly rise up to my knees so I'm eye-level with Kyler. I use my good hand to push against his chest, so he's forced to lie back. He does so carefully. I climb on top of him, straddling his waist, before he can guess my intent.

"Zara," he says my name in a rough, ragged tone, but doesn't ask me to get off. In fact, his hands go to my hips and grip them tightly.

"I want you to touch me."

"You are still hurt." There isn't too much protest in his voice though. It's gruff, like he's struggling to hold back his need.

My response is to roll my hips and grind myself against him. "I don't hurt, Kyler. I *ache*. For you."

He groans and shifts his hands until he's palming my ass. It's a start, but definitely not enough. I gently take my arm out of the sling, pull the length of fur over my head, and toss it off to the side. Needing more, I reach for his hand and slide it beneath my shirt to place it on my breast. I've never been generously endowed so most of the time I don't even bother with a bra. A fact I'm more than happy with at this very moment.

There's nothing sexier than seeing my man with a look of awe on his face. Okay, maybe getting felt up by said man is sexier, but it's a close race.

"Keeshla."

Nope, *that* is the sexiest thing, because the raw need in that single word has my panties soaking wet. "Touch me, Kyler. Any way you want."

It's as though I've unleashed a beast. He releases the grip he has on my other hip and palms both breasts. For a species whose females don't have them, he certainly knows what to do with a pair of boobs. A zing of pleasure zips through me as he rolls my nipples between his fingers and I rock my pelvis against his washboard stomach, trying to get some friction against my throbbing clit.

Kyler's hands are the perfect size, and he uses them exquisitely. I've never thought I was particularly sensitive, but holy shit, was I wrong. The pleasure from every caress, every nipple tweak, every gentle squeeze is amplified by a thousand. I could almost maybe orgasm from the tit play alone. Something that has never happened before.

A full body shudder wracks me and sends a sharp vibration to my lady parts. I roll my hips hard and gasp as a small tremor rips through my core. Fuck me. Score one for Kyler. The first man to make me lose my shit from second base alone. That's my mate.

Wanting him to get to this point with me, I lean slightly back and reach behind me to stroke his cock through his hide pants.

"Keeshla," he growls the word and the sensation travels through me.

Another ripple of pleasure hits my pussy, and I clench down as the feel of it registers. I trace the raised bumps that line his length, and dampness leaks through the fabric. This must the mating fluid my friends have talked about. It's some type of stimulant or aphrodisiac that makes amazing sex fucking explosive sex. My own wetness leaks out of me at the thought of something better than this. Because I already feel pretty damn good, and Kyler's not even inside me yet.

Together, we continue pleasuring each other—his hands on my breasts, and me stroking his cock—and I keep doing my best to rub my clit against his stomach. The pleasure is a slow build like a geyser that gains momentum with each tiny bubbling eruption.

"Fuck, you make me feel so good."

Out of nowhere, a bright light illuminates inside my chest. It warms me without burning, and the most powerful emotion travels through my entire body as though it's in my bloodstream. I glance down at my mate, and my heart nearly stops beating. His gaze is locked on me and the same light shines from within his eyes. He blinks and it's gone, but something else remains. I don't know how, but there's a knowledge inside me of exactly what it is. It's the love I still feeling coursing through my veins.

If there was any doubt before now that Kyler's my fated mate, it's been obliterated. A sense of peace fills me and on its heels is the strongest orgasm I've ever had. I cry out as I hit my peak and beneath me, he goes still, but the tendons in his neck tighten and flex. Warm liquid spreads across my hand that still holds his cock and my thighs are slick with my own wetness.

Kyler slides his hands down my ribs and settles them around my waist. Wrung out, I collapse onto his chest, ignoring the pain shooting through my arm that lands on the furs at his side. Both of us breathe heavily, gasping and pulling in air. My hair around my forehead and nape sticks to my skin from sweat. Beneath my cheek I can feel the pounding of his heart that I'm sure matches the rhythm of my own. It's like I've been running a race. We lay there until our breathing returns to normal and the ache in my arm can no longer be ignored.

I push myself upright and stretch for the discarded sling that's just out of reach. Kyler grabs it instead.

"Thanks."

Carefully, he helps me put my arm back in it and adjusts the fit. It's really hurting, but I don't regret what he and I just did. I move to stand, but he stops me with gentle hands on my face.

"I love you," Kyler says. "It is all right if you do not feel the same yet, but I could not go another beat of my heart without telling you."

Emotion wells up inside me. The only person who ever told me they loved me and meant it was Amelia. A part of me has always thought I'm unloveable. Even now, after hearing Kyler say it, I want to dismiss it. That he's only telling me that because I made him come. But the part of me that has hungered for it—craved it—wants to believe he truly means it.

I open my mouth to say…I don't know what, but he stops any words I might have uttered with a soft and gentle kiss. He draws back and climbs to his feet.

"Come, let us go to the healer's tent. I will tighten your splint again and get something for your pain." He holds out his hand and helps me up.

I'm not going to question how he knows I'm hurting, but I hold tightly to him as we leave my tent and step out into the sunshine.

CHAPTER 16

KYLER

The energy of the village is buzzing like a horde of mushkanja. It is always an exciting turn when the Bohnari visit. I leave the healer's tent where I have been since I tightened Zara's splint and gave her more burim root. She did not stay long, but instead, after a lingering kiss that set my mind at ease, went to go find her tribe sisters.

The scent of the midday meal sweeps in on the breeze, and I head for the central fire in search of my mate. The village is teeming with activity. Females and males—Tavikhi and humans alike—wander around. Some carry animal skins or food while others carry weapons. Kits race around, chasing each other, their laughter adding to the sounds of sparring that carries in from the training arena at the bottom of the rise.

It is easy to forget that only a few turns ago, a battle occurred, until my gaze sweeps side-to-side and takes in the burnt patches of land that spot the ground and the missing number of tents. A celebration of life was scheduled for tonight for those we lost in the Njeri attack, but it may be postponed until the Bohnari leave.

A small number of tribespeople gather around the central fire. Most of them attend the meal that will be served soon, but my eyes land on my mate. She sits with the shefira, who has one of the implements that Benham has been crafting for her to use to teach the kits how to read and write. I am not sure how useful this skill is, but London says that eventually, as the kits grow older, they will be able to carve stories of Tavikhi and Earth history on them.

As though sensing my gaze on her, Zara lifts her head and looks directly at me. A large smile blooms on her face like the petals of the trendafili flower opens for the sun. My soul light surges brightly within my chest and warmth spreads throughout me as I close the distance between us. Love fills my heart to nearly bursting.

I come to a stop in front of them and fist my chest. "Greetings, *keeshla*. Shefira."

Zara stands and kisses me. Her fingers slide through mine. I am pleased that she does not hide her affection. I wrap my tail around her waist. Unlike earlier, this is not a show of possession, but rather my own affection for her. When she smiles up at me, I would like to believe it is because she understands the difference.

"Hi, Kyler," London returns my greeting. "How are the injured warriors doing?"

"They are healing well. Several are anxious to leave and return to training, although it will still be at least two turns before I will release them. I do not want them to injure themselves again by sparring too soon."

She nods. "I'm so glad to hear that. Zander has been worried."

I glance around. It is not usual for the shefir to not be by his shefira's side during meal times. As though hearing my unasked question, London speaks again. "He'll be here soon. He and Alik are talking about whatever tribe leaders talk about."

Footsteps approach. As if conjured by her words, Zander and the Bohnari walk toward us. Zara squeezes my fingers and leans into me. I glance down at her and she rises up to press her lips against mine. She draws back, closes one eye before opening it again quickly, and turns toward the two males. I will have to ask her about this gesture when we are alone.

The moment Zander is within reach, his tail wraps around London and he greets her with a kiss and whispered words. My gaze is on Alik and for beat, I am almost certain a flash of longing crosses his face, but it disappears so swiftly, I must be mistaken.

"Shefira," the Bohnari greets London with a bow when she finally turns to face him.

London nods.

"Greetings, Kyler." Zander fists his chest and I return it.

"Healer." the Bohnari leader dips his head and his gaze shifts to my mate. "Zara."

"Alik," she says, but her tone is neutral and I try not to gloat.

"The rest of the Bohnari should be arriving soon and then the celebration will begin," Zander announces. "We will be celebrating not only our allies, but also our fallen tribe brothers and sisters."

"My people are honored to be included in celebrating the lives of yours. Thank you for allowing us to be a part of it. No doubt they will be missed by all." Alik displays a far more serious demeanor than I have witnessed from him before.

Perhaps there is more to the Bohnari than I previously thought.

"Many thanks." Zander fists his chest and Alik does the same.

"I will clean up in the river while I await the arrival of the rest of my crew. Shefira." He bows at London and then turns and walks away.

"I'm going to take this back to our tent." London holds up the clay implement. "We'll be right back."

She and Zander depart as well.

"Come, let us sit." Without removing my tail from around her waist, Zara and I move to one of the carved wooden seats near the fire. "How was your visit with your tribe sisters?"

"Good. After what happened to me, we needed to spend the time together. It really kind of hit us how lucky I was you guys found me. It could have been so much worse." She shudders.

I do not want to even consider any other outcome.

"How is your arm feeling?" It is the closest I can get to acknowledging what happened between us in her tent without asking outright if Zara regrets what we did. I am not sure I could handle her saying yes.

"It constantly aches, but most of the time it's better than not." She bites her lip. "What did Alik mean when he said their healer can repair it?"

"I am unsure." One of the things we trade with the Bohnari is kanet. It is nothing more than a basic plant that grows deep in the forest, but according to their healer, they use it for healing. Except it is entirely useless as nothing more than vegetation on Tavikh. "But I will take you to their ship when it arrives if you wish. If the Bohnari can do something to heal it, I believe it is a good thing."

"You'll come with me then?"

The hope in Zara's eyes is nearly my undoing. The fact that she wishes for me to be at her side means everything to me. "Of course."

She loops her arm around mine and leans her head on my shoulder. "Thank you."

As we sit there, more and more tribespeople arrive—including the elders, who tend to stay near their own group of tents—and soon the midday meal is well underway. Her tribe sisters and their mates join us and the females talk and laugh with each other. Alik sits with several unmated warriors. I observe him several times watching all the mated humans, and the same look I'd witnessed earlier crosses his face, but when our eyes meet, his expression clears. I sympathize. They do not worship the same goddess as we do, but I pray to Deeka that their males are able to find their own mates.

Slowly, people finish eating and drop their vessels off at the fire for washing. Throughout the meal, Zara has touched me often. Not all of them feel purposeful. Often her thigh would brush against mine. Or her arm when she leaned forward to speak to Remi who sat on my other side. Whether intentional or not, each touch sent pleasure straight to my cock.

I have just emptied my vessel when a sound reaches me. Conversations halt and heads lift toward the sky. A shadow appears through the clouds growing larger with every beat until, at last, it breaks through to expose the Bohnari ship. All eyes observe it as it floats through the air, drawing closer to the earth, until it disappears behind the trees outside of the village borders to land in the large bari field that lies beyond.

"Whoa," Zara exclaims. "That was nothing like the ship that brought us here."

The human's transport ship is more than three times the size of the Bohnari's, but that is because the smaller of the two is built for only a few warriors. She would be even more surprised to see Alik's shuttle. It is sized to hold only a single warrior.

"I wonder if they'll let us have a tour," Eloise says. "I'm curious to see the inside."

As someone who traveled the stars before crash landing on Tavikh, it makes sense that she would be interested in the interior workings of the Bohnari vessel.

"I'd be down for a tour," Remi proclaims.

"Me too," the shefira says.

"I want to visit their med bay," Sage adds.

The only one who remains silent is Maeve.

Zara chuckles. "Sounds like we might all be making a field trip."

"'Field trip'?" That is not a term that translates.

"It's an old Earth thing. It was when a group of people, usually students—children—traveled together to visit a particular place."

"I see." It is an interesting custom of humans to come up with odd names for things.

Alik approaches and comes to a stop before Zander. "I will greet my brothers and return with them."

Zydon rises. "I will accompany you if that is all right. I have been looking forward to speaking with Horek again."

"He will be glad to see you." With a fist to his chest, Alik turns away and he and Zydon head for the main entrance of the village.

I face Zara. "Once the Bohnari returns and brings his tribe brothers back, we can go to the ship and meet with the healer. He most often remains aboard."

"Okay."

Normally, the tribespeople would have all dispersed by now to go about their day, but not this time. Only the few whose task it is to clean up after the meal have left with all the eating and drinking vessels to head for the river to wash them all. They will return though. It is a day of celebration and rest for everyone else.

CHAPTER 17

Zara

Only a couple days ago I swore I wasn't leaving the village borders ever again. Yet here I am about to not only step foot outside of them, but to enter a ship belonging to aliens I've never met before today. The Tavikhi know and trust them, but that doesn't mean a person can't betray that trust on a dime. I should know.

My stomach is all tied up in knots as Kyler and I walk past the two Tavikhi warriors guarding the main entrance. Six of the Bohnari people returned with Alik and Zydon. Each male resembled their leader in coloring and size, but their horns were all slightly different and each had their own distinct facial features in the same way Tavikhi vary from one another.

"Is all well, *keeshla*?" Kyler asks the farther we get from the safety of the village. Which is ridiculous, because it's not as though I can't still see it.

"I'm just a little nervous, I guess."

Kyler comes to a halt and brings me with him. He palms my cheek. "We do not have to go if you are uncomfortable. Nothing says we cannot turn around and walk back into the village."

"No." I release a heavy sigh. "If their healer can fix my arm so I'm back to normal again, then I want to do it. It's only been four days, and I'm already over this shit."

His gaze bores into me. "If you are sure."

Yes. No. Not really.

I take his hand. "C'mon, let's go."

Together we continue traipsing through the trees where small animals scurry away from the sound of our footsteps, and out the other side. I finally get an up close and personal look at the Bohnari ship. It's a matte black so dark and flat it doesn't even reflect the light from the sun. In fact, it's almost as though it absorbs it. What it lacks in color it makes up for in sleek, sharp lines.

At our approach, there's a slight hissing sound, and a ramp lowers at the back of the ship. Either we were expected—which is the most likely scenario since Alik was here a short time ago—or they have surveillance equipment that spotted us which activated it. I'm not sure which one I prefer. As though sensing my trepidation, Kyler squeezes my hand in reassurance.

We head toward the metal slope, but before we reach it, a shadow along the surface grows until a pair of black boots appear followed by legs encased in black pants, then a torso in a matching shirt that molds to the owner's body, until finally the person is fully exposed. Unlike Alik's grin which was purely flirtatious, this guy's is sincerely welcoming. His eyes light up with excitement.

"Kyler, my friend. How wonderful to see you again." The Bohnari jogs down the ramp toward us.

"Vornak." There's an echoing pleasure in my mate's tone. "Welcome back."

The two males clasp forearms, and the Bohnari pounds Kyler on the shoulder before his gaze travels over his mating marks. If anything, his grin widens, and then he glances over at me and down to where my mate still holds my hand.

"Vornak, this is Zara. My *keeshla*."

The male bows and crosses his fist over his chest. "It is an honor to meet the mate of this fine, worthy male. Congratulations to both of you. It would appear as though the gods and goddesses are smiling down on both the Tavikhi and Bohnari. I, too, have found a mate after all this time. There is hope for our people yet."

"By Deeka's flame, that is wonderful news," Kyler says and I sense his genuine happiness.

"Come, I will introduce you. She awaits in the med room."

The tension that had been wound up inside me loosens. Vornak seems friendly enough, and I don't get any weird vibes from Kyler about him. He truly likes this guy. Plus, he can't be that bad if he has a wife. Right? We climb the incline that bounces a little with each step, and the metal clinks under my shoes. The interior is far less dark than it appeared from the outside.

It smells like metal and fuel. We traverse several hallways behind Vornak until he comes to a stop in front of a door. He places his palm on the biometric reader, and it slides open bringing with it a brightly lit room. Kyler and I step inside. We both come to an abrupt halt.

"Holy fucking shit. You're human."

The woman laughs and hops down off the counter to land with a metallic thunk. She approaches with an outstretched hand. "Hi there. I'm Johnna, Vornak's mate."

I shake it in numbed shock. Of all the things I could have expected today, meeting another human wasn't anywhere on the list. Then her uncommon name hits me. "Wait. Did you say Johnna?"

She cocks her head and wrinkles her forehead. "Yeah."

"Do you know a woman named Eloise?"

Johnna's eyes widen. "She was my bunkmate on the terraforming ship we both worked on. Why?"

"She's *here*. On Tavikh." I turn and lightly smack Kyler's chest. "This is Eloise's friend that she's told us about. Oh my god, she's going to shit kittens."

The other woman stumbles back a couple steps and Vornak rushes forward to catch her in his arms. She glances up at him with a hand on his chest and tears in her eyes. "She's alive. All this time, I've prayed Eloise made it somewhere safe and she did."

"Yes, she did, my heart's fire." He kisses her on the forehead, and she leans into him with eyes closed and a tear slides down her cheek.

The sight of it chokes me up a little. Kyler's tail wraps around my waist and he takes my hand again, threading his fingers through mine. Several seconds pass before Johnna draws back from Vornak and faces me. "Will you take me to her when you guys are finished?"

"Of course. She's going to be so happy to see you." Eloise has talked about her friend often and how badly she wished she knew she was okay.

"No more than I am."

"Alik said you can heal my mate," Kyler says to Vornak, bringing us back to the main reason we're here.

He nods. "Of course. Come."

I glance up at Kyler before he releases me, and I walk forward to where the Bohnari healer has moved next to a machine that looks like a giant egg lying sideways with a glass top. He presses a button and the glass lifts with a faint hydraulic sound.

"You will need to remove the sling and splint before entering the med pod. If you lie on your back inside, the scanners will assess the damage to your arm. Once it is finished, you may feel some heat and minor tingling as it knits the bone or bones back together."

I swallow and glance at Kyler. I've never been claustrophobic, but the thought of being stuck in that thing that reminds me a bit too much of a coffin makes me want to hurl. Already my palm is clammy and my heart thumps madly.

"Hey," Johnna says and I turn my head toward her. "I know we're strangers and there's no reason to trust me, but I promise this thing works magic. When I crash landed on Bohna, I almost died. Vornak saved me. You'll barely feel a thing."

I shift my gaze to Kyler.

"I will be by your side the entire time you are in there if you want to remain," he says. "If not, we will return to the village. It is whatever you are most comfortable with doing."

For twenty-seven years every decision of my life had been made for me. What time I went to bed. What I ate. What I wore. Who my friends were even though none of them were real friends. It wasn't until I learned the truth about what happened to Amelia did I start to rebel and make my own decisions. Most of them were pretty shitty ones that led to nothing but trouble, including the entire reason I'm on Tavikh in the first place.

Although, aside from getting kidnapped, life here hasn't been that bad. It brought me a husband—a mate—after all. The fact that Kyler isn't pressuring me one way or another, but is leaving the choice to proceed or not up to me means more than he'll ever know.

I swallow. "Let's do this."

Vornak nods. "I will let your mate remove your splint and help you into the pod."

Kyler approaches and the Bohnari healer returns to Johnna's side. I stare up at my mate as he helps me out of my sling.

"Thank you for being here."

He carefully unwinds the sinew keeping the twigs and branches strapped around my arm. "There is no place else I would rather be. You are my *keeshla*. The other half of my soul. Where you go, I go."

Son of a bitch. He's going to make me cry. I sniff back the tears and swing my leg up into the coffin egg. Kyler takes my hand and I use him for balance and to push myself back until my entire body is inside. I don't take my eyes off him as I lay back and rest my head in the gel cushion. Our eyes stay locked together even when Vornak lowers the lid and encloses me inside. The sharp sound of a lock engaging makes me flinch. I watch every breath my man takes and match my breathing to his. He's far calmer than I am.

Like Vornak said, a blue line I can only assume is the scanner runs over my body from head to toe. I hear a few beeps now and then, but otherwise it's completely quiet. Eerily so. It's like I'm inside a type of sensory deprivation tank. There's another beep and then the warmth seeps into my arm. Sure enough a tingling sensation follows right on its heels. It almost tickles and I try not to shift or move in any way. It would be just my luck that the machine knits my bones together all wonky.

I don't know how long I lie here, but finally my arm cools, and the tingling stops. The same blue light from before runs over me, and a single beep sounds. Then the lock disengages and with a pneumatic hiss, it slowly flips open. Kyler places a hand behind my back and helps me sit up. I swing my legs over the side and let them dangle.

Vornak comes over and gestures to my arm lying in my lap. "May I?"

I nod and he picks it up. Gently, he prods it, and I wait for the pain, but there's nothing. Not even a twinge.

"Wiggle your fingers for me, please."

I do what he asks and even twist my forearm side to side without prompting. Nothing. Well, hot damn. "It feels great. Not a single ache or anything. It's like it was never broken."

"Push against my hand," Vornak prompts and holds up his arm.

I move to do what he says, but Kyler gives me his palm instead. I blink and glance at the Bohnari healer. who smirks and steps back. I lay my hand on my mate's and gently push. When nothing happens, I press harder, bracing for the stabbing pain, but there's nothing except the pressure of my palm against his. I relax my muscles and thread my fingers through his with a smile.

"Good as new."

"I am glad, *keeshla*."

Kyler helps me hop down and we turn toward Vornak and Johnna. "Thank you for everything."

"It's my pleasure," he says. "If there is nothing more I may help you with, my heart's fire is anxious to be reunited with her friend."

"Absolutely." We all head toward the med room exit. "I can't wait to see Eloise's face when she sees you."

Kyler and I leave the Bohnari ship and make our way back to the village with Johnna and Vornak. The past two days don't feel real. How many people can say they not only met a new alien species, but also had a broken bone fixed by some high-tech machine in something like fifteen minutes? Even better? I had a hot make-out session with my man who gave me one of the best orgasms I've ever had. God knows how much better it'll be when we actually have sex.

Five days ago, I thought I was going to die. I glance over at Kyler and then up to the sky.

Thanks, Lia. You were right. He came.

CHAPTER 18

KYLER

Never have I before seen the healing technology that Vornak possesses at work. He has shown and explained his machine to me in the past, but I could not comprehend how it functioned. I still do not, but I am fascinated. I have never questioned the Bohnari's need for kanet. I was only told that it offered special healing properties that were not available on their own planet and they would be happy to trade whatever it is we wish for it. If they have the kind of machine that can heal broken bones, what use do they have for a simple plant? I find myself curious.

I am grateful for Vornak's help in healing Zara. Nothing pleases me more than to see her healthy and without pain. Except perhaps to see her own happiness at being whole again. The sounds of the celebration grow louder the closer we get to the village. No doubt the elders have brought out their special brew and the drinking has begun. It will go long into the night as we have much to celebrate.

"Sounds like they started the party without us," Zara jokes.

"Do not worry *keeshla*. There will be plenty of time to enjoy the festivities."

"I'm ready for some of that delicious alcohol." She makes a noise of delight. "I'll warn you ahead of time, Johnna, it has a nice kick to it."

Vornak's mate laughs. "Thanks for the heads up. If it's anything like the Xurxell beer Eloise and I used to drink, I'll make sure to pace myself."

The guards at the gate greet us with a fist over their chest, but their eyes widen at the sight of us returning with an unfamiliar human female. I fist my chest as well and we walk through the entrance and make our way toward the central fire that burns brightly and is surrounded already by Bohnari, Tavikhi, and humans.

Our presence catches the attention of Zander who breaks away from London to come toward us. She turns her head to watch him and spots us, because she waves with a smile. Zara waves back with her newly repaired arm. The shefir reaches our small party and we come to a stop. He salutes us and then clasps arms with the Bohnari healer.

"Welcome back, Vornak. It is always good to see another of our Bohnari brothers."

"Thank you, Shefir," he replies and then places an arm around his female. "This is my mate, J—"

"Johnna?" Eloise tears away from the group, her eyes shimmering.

"Johnna," she screams and breaks into a run.

"Oh my god, Eloise." The two females collide with their arms wrapped tightly around each other. Both of them sob.

Zedam and Vornak go to their mates' sides while the females celebrate their reunion. Beside me, Zara sniffs. I glance down at her and she swipes away the tears in her eyes. She lifts her gaze to mine and smiles. Human emotions are often confusing.

"Happy tears?"

She nods. "Happy. So, so happy."

I twine my tail around her waist and we join all of our tribespeople and the Bohnari at the fire. We have much to celebrate this day.

The barest edge of the sun lingers over the hilltop, fighting to remain visible in the sky, but within several beats of my heart, it is defeated and disappears completely, leaving the two moons as champions. As the evening has progressed, the number of tribespeople has dwindled. First with the elders as they made their way to their own tents, followed by the kits whose complaints were audible even as they stepped into their own dwellings.

Zara and all her tribe sisters—as well as several more of the humans—have been celebrating with something they call dancing and Eloise has gifted us with the sound of her voice in what she calls singing. She has attempted to teach Zedam this thing and to the surprise of everyone, he produces a melodious noise that blends perfectly with his *keeshla's*. The other humans often join in and it becomes clear that not all of them are as gifted as Eloise and Zedam.

It is a joyous night. The elders' brew has been passed around many times and its effects are more than obvious. Words are slurred. Laughter is louder. Movement is unsteadier. It has been since before the sun descended that Zander called out the names of all our fallen tribe brothers and sisters and each received their own battle cry from everyone. The sounds echoed for many beats before fading away.

Zara stumbles over to me on the far side of the circle with laughter spilling from her lips. She collides against my chest and wraps her arms around me. With her touching me, our surroundings disappear and it is as if only she and I exist.

"Mmmm, you smell good. Like eulyptus but mished— mixed"—she shakes her head and wrinkles her nose— "with something sweet. It makes me want to lick you to see if you taste as yummy." As if proving her point, her tongue runs across my flesh.

I should not grow hard that fast, but I do. "And how do I taste?"

Zara lifts only her eyes as she continues licking and nibbling my skin. "Delicious. I bet your cock tastes even better. Less go back to our tent, so I can see."

Mating fluid erupts from my nodes and a shudder runs down my spine as she rubs herself against me. An image of my mate between my thighs and her mouth on me nearly has me coming in my leg coverings. I must steel myself against the onslaught of pleasure though, because as much I love the idea of Zara pleasuring me in that way, I cannot. Not while she is under the influence of the elders' brew.

"As much as I want to have my *keeshla* taste me, it will have to wait for another night. When you are not affected by drink." No worthy warrior would take advantage of their female while she is in this state.

She blinks multiple times, as though surprised by my rejection, and then stares. "Bryce didn't care that I was drunk."

I cock my head and go still. "Who is Bryce?"

"My boyfriend. *Ex*-boyfriend," Zara emphasizes. "Although he was a pretty shitty boyfriend."

"You had a mate?"

She rattles her head. "He wasn't my mate. Just a guy I dated."

I do not understand the difference. She must sense my continued confusion even in her altered state because she sighs. "A boyfriend is a guy you like and spend time with in the hopes you both fall in love with each other and then marry—become mates."

"And you wanted to become mates with this…Bryce?" A pain stabs my heart.

Zara raises and lowers a shoulder. "I thought I did. Before I found out he was a raging cocksucker."

"He also tastes cocks? Males do this?"

She bursts out laughing. "No, he didn't taste cocks, although, yes, some males do. A cocksucker just means Bryce was a giant piece of shit."

Ah, yes excrement is a word I know since she favors using it. If I did not already hate this male for being her 'boyfriend', I would hate him for the pain he has obviously caused her. If this Bryce—his name alone makes my blood boil with rage —took advantage of Zara when she had imbibed on human brew, then he is worthless and without honor.

"Did he force you?" A bigger part of me does not want to know the answer, because not being able to avenge my *keeshla* will eat away at me.

Zara laughs again, but it is filled with bitterness. She also sounds surprisingly alert. "He didn't have to force me. I stupidly believed all his flattery and smooth words. That should have been my first clue, but I was so lonely I ate up every compliment he gave me."

This is not a conversation meant to have out in the open. "Will you come with me to my tent and tell me what happened?"

There is a short pause before she nods. "You might as well find out now before I fall too much harder for you and you realize I'm not the kind of mate you want."

My heart leaps at Zara's words. Does this mean she is closer to loving me? And have I not shown her enough that she is the perfect mate for me? If she believes I would not want her, no matter what she tells me, then I have done a poor job of showing her my feelings. I will remedy that as soon as possible. After tonight, she will never doubt my love.

I thread my fingers through hers and together we leave the celebration for my dwelling. It is the first time Zara will have entered it. I have not slept there since before she was taken, although I have returned to wash up and put on clean leg coverings. We come to a stop in front of it and I swing the door flap to the side for her to enter. I grab the torch from the ground and bring it—as well as its light—in with me so we are both able to see better.

While she slowly walks around to take in my home, I apply the flame to the wood in the center pit. Once it smolders and catches fire, I stab the torch upright into the ground beside it. I observe Zara, curious to know what her thoughts are. She finally finishes her inspection and turns to me. My tent is much smaller than hers since it has always only housed me, but I have done my best to make it feel welcoming to visitors.

"You have a really nice place," she says, and the tension I'd been holding eases away knowing that she is pleased with it.

From the wooden beams I have several bundles of dried zambak to give a pleasant fragrance to the air and there are two carved seats. Before he died, Baba crafted a sleeping platform for me that sits a knee's height off the ground and is covered with many plush furs that once belonged to him and Nene.

"I am glad you like it since I hope that it will become your home."

Zara wrings her hands together in a nervous gesture I have never witnessed from her before. I close the distance between us and take them between mine, squeezing gently to try and ease her mind. Nothing she tells me will change how I feel. But I do not believe words will reassure her. Only my actions will.

"Come, let us sit and you can tell me your story." I guide her to the sleeping platform since it is more comfortable than the hard seats.

She sits, scoots all the way back to the middle, and folds her legs. When she pats the empty space in front of her, I move there and mimic her pose. We sit in silence. I can tell Zara is gathering her thoughts so I remain quiet and patient. Trust must be earned and I am willing to give her all the time she needs.

CHAPTER 19

ZARA

God, this is harder than I thought it would be. I'm still feeling the slight effects of the alcohol, but now it's just a heavy buzz. It's funny how talking about my greatest mistake is enough to sober me up a bit. Deep down I know I'm not to blame—that I'm the victim—but in my head I can still hear the whisper of Clifton Black's voice telling me this is all my fault.

When Kyler continues to sit in silence, I understand that he'll wait as long as he needs to for me to start talking. It's what actually gives me the courage to speak.

"It's probably best to start from the beginning." I let out a deep breath. "Neither of my parents were nice people. I'm not sure why they even had children in the first place, because they made it clear that both Amelia—my sister—and I were nothing more than an inconvenience. Lia became not only my best friend, but also my mother. If it wasn't for her, I wouldn't know what love is."

There's still that void inside me from her loss, but somehow lately, it doesn't seem quite as big.

"When I was about Talek's age, my sister killed herself. I lost the only person who ever loved me and I was so young I didn't understand why," my voice cracks and I clear my throat. "At least not until almost two years ago. That's when I found out all those years ago she'd been… raped—forced—by her boyfriend. It's why she did what she did."

It's been eighteen years since she's been gone, and the truth is still hard to say out loud.

"You told me that you wished the male who hurt your sister had died instead of her," Kyler reminds me. "I too wish this for you. Any male who hurts a female in that way deserves to be struck down. I am sorry that did not happen and that your sister was taken from you."

I reach out for his hands and hold them tight. "Thank you. For saying that."

He nods and I continue.

"Anyway, when I found out the truth, and worse, that my parents had been paid by her rapist to keep it quiet, I started to rebel and act out. They never cared about Amelia or me, so why should I care about them?" My voice is raised in anger, but I bring it down. "I started dating Bryce because I knew they didn't approve of him. He was part of the upper tier—the rich—but his family didn't have nearly the wealth mine did. Clifton and Priscilla Black are nothing if not pretentious snobs. He gave me all the attention I'd been missing out on after Amelia was gone. I'd been starved for it and I drank it all in, ignoring all the warning signs."

I laugh bitterly because, in that regard, maybe it was my fault.

"One night we went to a party, and I had a lot to drink. Not enough to be completely incapacitated, but definitely inebriated. I'm not sure if Bryce knew that it was the anniversary of Amelia's death or not, but looking back, I suspect he did." It makes sense. "He coaxed me upstairs to an empty bedroom and we started making out. Of course, things escalated and before long we were having sex. It wasn't our first time ever, but it was the first time since he'd told me he loved me."

Kyler stiffens but doesn't say anything. I kind of wish he would. At least so I know that he hasn't changed his mind or feelings about me yet. Of course, I haven't even gotten to the worst part, so maybe it's a good thing.

"After it was over, I fell asleep, or passed out more likely. When I woke up, Bryce was gone. There wasn't a single trace of him. I got dressed to go look for him, but when I got downstairs, everyone was staring at me. Laughing. Whispering to each other. One of Bryce's friends walked by and smacked my ass. He said 'good show'. I had no idea what he was talking about." I shake my head at how stupid I'd been. "I finally left the party and went home. When I got there and looked at my comm, I saw the notification. A link to some website. I never should have clicked on it, but I did. There it was, right in front of me. Evidence of what my rebelling had led to. My boyfriend—the guy who'd only the day before told me he loved me—had videotaped us having sex without my knowledge or consent and live-streamed it so every single person at that party saw it. Not only that, but the video had made its way to the parents of those at the party, including my own. Apparently, Clifton had humiliated Bryce's dad during some business deal which led him to leave his family. I was payback."

I meet Kyler's eyes and they have changed color. In fact, the yellow of them has almost completely disappeared and only the purple-black remains. I've never seen that happen to any Tavikhi before and have no idea what it means. Is he so disgusted by what I did that he doesn't want me anymore? My gut aches and I want to cry, but I do what I've done for twenty-seven years and hide my emotions.

"You asked me why I came to Tavikh. Well, that's why. After the video went public, my parents disowned me. Kicked me out. I left with a single bag full of clothes and without a credit to my name. When we were younger, Amelia and I always talked about leaving the upper tier and going to some made-up place with a cute house and a yard filled with pretty flowers. When I saw the sign about leaving Earth for Tavikh, I just knew it was a message from my sister." I manage a short laugh. "Imagine my surprise when I landed here and didn't get either of those things."

It was meant as a joke and to get at least maybe a smile out of Kyler. Except he remains rigid and his eyes are still more black than yellow. He doesn't crack a grin or let out a small chuckle. His jaw clenches so hard I can see the muscles along it shift. Only briefly during my story did his hands tighten on mine, but it lasted barely a second. That's the biggest movement he's made the entire time and it's starting to make me nervous.

"Are you going to say anything? You're freaking me out a little here."

Kyler releases my hands and climbs off the bed. He paces the tent with his fists opening and closing every two or three steps. I track his path back and forth and the knot in my stomach grows. He comes to a stop in the middle of the place and stares at me.

"If I could travel to your planet and kill that dishonorable male with my bare hands, I would," he growls from deep within his chest, his black eyes darkening more.

"What?" I mean, I heard him, but the words haven't processed yet. Until they do.

"Are those the kind of people who live on Earth? Babas and Nenes who would treat their kits so horribly? Almost mates who cause so much pain and suffering they no longer want to live? Or who are so cowardly as to use a female for revenge?" Kyler's rage vibrates the ground he stands on. "It is no wonder you wanted to be free of them. How could anyone who knows you not see how courageous and kind and loving you are? How could they dare do anything to hurt you? I have never had hate in my heart until now. I would destroy each and every one of those who have done something to dishonor you."

With every word he speaks, the tension bleeds from me. In its place is a mishmash of emotions. I can count on one hand the number of times I've cried in the last eighteen years. Except I can't stop the tears that have welled in my eyes from falling. I had hoped Kyler wouldn't blame me for what happened and that he would understand it wasn't my fault, but never in my wildest dreams would I have expected so much anger on my behalf. No one has ever defended me so fiercely. Threatened to actually *kill* someone who hurt me.

Every wall—every defense—that I've kept carefully locked around my heart crumbles. Even when I felt Kyler's soul light join with me, I didn't let it take hold, because I didn't truly think someone could love me. The person who has always been so unloved. So unloveable. Except now, I embrace the light that's been flickering inside me and I make a vow to never, ever let it—let *him*—go.

I make my way off the bed as well and go to him. He stares intently down at me with eyes still blazing with rage. I loop my hands around the back of his neck and pull his head down toward me. I rise up on my tippy toes and our mouths meet in a perfect kiss. Perfect because it is filled with the purest of emotions. Love. I put everything I am and want to be in the kiss and hope Kyler understands what I'm saying without the three words I'm too over-whelmed with to express verbally. This is more than love. This is adoration. It's he-is-my-world-and-I-can't-live-without-him.

His hands go around my hips and he lifts me. My legs wrap around his waist and my arms tighten around him.

Without breaking the kiss, he walks us over to the bed and gently lays me down on it. Kyler's body covers mine and he settles between my thighs. My hands slide slowly up and down his back, memorizing every crevice and ridge along the way. His skin is like soft, buttered leather and I'll never get enough of it.

I want him to know what this means to me. Touching him. Having him touch me. I clutch at Kyler's shoulders and tug slightly. He releases my mouth and stares down at me.

"For as long as Amelia's been gone, I haven't liked people touching me. Not…him. Not even my new sisters here on Tavikh. But it's never been like that with you. Even in the beginning. It's like my mind, body, and heart knew it belonged with you and that you would take care with them. Having you touch me every day for the rest of my life will never be enough."

"*Keeshla,*" Kyler rasps out in a gravelly tone that vibrates straight to my clit.

"Make love to me. Please. I need you."

He hesitates. "I do not want to take advantage of your vulnerable state."

If I hadn't finally accepted that I loved him, I would now. I cradle his head between my palms and stroke his cheeks with my thumbs. "You aren't taking advantage. You're showing your mate what it's like to truly be in love."

Kyler studies my face and I stare deeply into his eyes, my heart and soul completely exposed to him. I don't want to hold anything back. Not anymore.

CHAPTER 20

KYLER

My beautiful *keeshla* loves me. She has not said those exact words, but I see them in her eyes. The reflection of my soul light shines from her lovely orbs and emits the same warmth that spreads throughout my chest. Zander and the rest of the mated males say that we share our soul light with our human mates and when they possess our other half, that is how we know they have fallen in love with us. It is clear from the light shining from Zara's eyes that half of my soul belongs to her.

My heart swells and I lean down and bring my mouth to hers. The scent of her arousal fills the air and the taste of the brew she drank earlier crosses my tongue. My mating nodes continue to leak their fluid and I rock my pelvis against my mate's knowing that soon I will be inside the warm heat of her cunt. I slide my hand beneath her chest covering to palm her chest mound. It is just as sweet and perfect as I remember it being and the tip is hard beneath my fingertips.

I roll the stiff bud between them in the way Zara enjoyed the last time and she arches her back, pressing her chest mound harder against my hand.

"Kyler, please," she begs. "I want to feel you without anything between us."

I rise up and before I can do anything else, she yanks her covering up and over her head. At last, I get my first look at her naked flesh. The round center of her chest mounds are a darker color than the skin surrounding it and the hardened tips resemble small pebbles.

"By Deeka's flame, you are perfection." I am in stunned awe of my *keeshla's* beauty.

Zara's cheeks darken to a shade similar to the circles of her chest mounds. Sage has said the color change is called a blush.

"No one has ever looked at me like you do," she says.

"That is because they are all fools. I am your mate. Of course I will look upon you as though you are the most stunning creature in existence. It is because you are. There is nothing and no one who surpasses your beauty in my eyes."

She sniffs. "Goddamn it. You're not supposed to be this fucking sweet. You're far too nice for someone like me."

"I am just the right amount of sweet and nice and perfect for someone like you. Deeka knew that we were meant to be together and that we complement each other and bring out the best in one another. I have always trusted the path she has placed me on, because I knew that one day she would bring you into my life. I only needed to remain patient, and I would be rewarded."

Zara scans my face and then she pulls me down to her and latches her lips onto mine. I let her deepen the kiss and our tongues twine together. Our hands roam, learning all the places on each other's body that brings us the most plea-sure. When she reaches between us and strokes my cock through my leg coverings, I nearly release my seed. It takes every ounce of strength I have to not lose control. I want to come inside her. I want to make a kit with her.

"Take off your pants," Zara demands.

I roll to my side and shed my leg coverings. She does the same and her musky scent grows stronger. My mouth waters with the need to taste her cunt. I have wanted to explore her since the first time I saw her bare in the forest.

"May I taste you?"

She bites her lip and slowly nods. I do not waste time in case she changes her mind. In a single beat of my heart, I put my mouth on her. It is the most divine flavor to ever touch my tongue. With every lick, I listen for the sounds Zara makes, and what makes her shift and press herself upward, as though searching for more of what I'm giving her. She gasps and moans, and wetness flows out of her to pool beneath her. I lap as much of it up as I can, drinking her down, not wanting to lose a single drop.

I encounter the entrance of her cunt and slide my tongue deep inside as far as I can go. Zara bucks her hips and cries out in ecstasy. I remove it and replace it with my finger so that I can play with the inflamed nub at the top of her slit where she is the most sensitive. In and out I thrust the digit, mimicking the movement my cock will make once I am inside her. She spears her fingers through my hair and clutches tightly at my head, holding me to her.

A second finger joins the first and I stretch her. Prepare her. I am of average size, but my *keeshla* is one of the smallest females and I do not want to hurt her. Zara is wet and my mating fluid will provide even more wetness, but she needs to be ready to accept me.

I suck on the hardened pebble above her cunt and add a third finger. Her body goes tense, and she clenches down, pulling them deeper inside her and a scream is ripped from her throat. It is a scream of pleasure and the sweetest sound to touch my ears. Dampness coats her skin and tiny strands of hair stick to her brow.

Spasms continue rippling through her cunt until finally they come to a stop. Zara's eyes flutter open and she gazes down at me still between her thighs. Her smile is one of a satisfied female.

"I want you inside me," she says roughly.

I crawl up her body and place my cock at her entrance. Without taking my eyes off hers, I slowly slide into her cunt, my mating fluid easing the way. A groan rumbles up from my chest at how tightly she squeezes me. Once I am as deep inside her as I can get, I hold myself still and savor the feel of her warm sheath wrapped around me.

Zara strokes my face. "I love you. I'm not just saying that because of the sex either. I mean, it's great and all—amazing, in fact—but that's not why I'm saying it. I can't not say it. Kyler, you're everything I never knew I wanted in a husband. In a mate. Thank you for showing me what true and unconditional love feels like. And for teaching me how to love you back."

"My *keeshla*. You have made me the happiest male on Tavikh. My soul light shines only for you and will continue to do so long after I pass into the lands of the goddess."

Zara rises up and claims my mouth with a kiss. I swipe my tongue inside and my cock mimics the movement. My pace increases and I go deeper with each thrust. I can feel my release coming and I do not know how to stop it. Needing my mate to reach her peak again before I do, I reach between us and circle that sensitive nub the way I discovered she loves the most.

Soon Zara's pleasure swells and crests again and she cries out my name. That is all it takes to trigger my own release. My seed explodes from my cock and fills her up. I say a prayer to Deeka that it takes and soon her belly will swell with my kit. Exhausted, I collapse on top of her, doing my best to keep most of my weight off. She clutches me tighter and I sink deeper against her.

"I am too heavy for you." I try to push myself up, but Zara will not let me go.

"No, you're not. Just lie here for a little bit."

Careful not to hurt her, I remain where I am as she strokes her fingertips up and down my back and our breathing slows. My cock softens within her and finally she shifts and loosens her hold on me. I roll and bring her with me so she lies on my chest. We are still connected in the most intimate way. Peace settles in my heart and my soul light still glows with warmth.

Zara turns her head so her cheek is pressed against me and her breath glides across my flesh. My arms hold her and my tail loops around her leg. She breathes out a soft sigh.

"When I was with the Njeri and unconscious most of the time, I talked to Amelia," she says quietly. "It kept the insanity away. Which probably doesn't make any sense, considering it sounds insane that I was talking to a dead person. Even worse that she actually answered me back."

I let my fingers glide up and down Zara's back now. "I do not think it sounds insane. There were times right after the death of my baba and nene that I spoke with them and they with me. It brought me great comfort for a short time."

She lifts her head and brings her hands beneath her chin and rests it on them.

"I tried escaping a few times and I never made it easy on them. It's why that dickhead hit me so often and then tied me up. Well, also because I kicked him in the balls, and god it felt good." Zara chuckles and then sobers. "The last time I talked to Amelia she told me to please stop fighting back. I said something really shitty to her, but she forgave me because that's the kind of person she was. Never held a grudge or had anything bad to say about anyone."

"Did she tell you why she wanted you to stop fighting?"

Zara murmurs an assent. "Her exact words were 'because he's coming'. When I saw your mating marks for the first time, I thought I was hallucinating. I didn't think that they were because of me. Until you almost called me *keeshla* . I asked myself if you were who she meant when she said 'he's coming'. Do you know when I *knew* it was you?"

I shake my head.

"When we were walking back to the village tonight from the Bohnari ship after my arm had been healed," Zara says. "The whole time I was lying in that machine, not once did you leave my side. You stayed there watching over me, and then, when it was finished, the way you stepped in front of Vornak and made sure his machine had done its job and healed me, I was pretty certain. But the absolute rightness of it hit me while we walked. I almost swore I could hear Lia whisper "Told you so" in my ear."

"Your sister was right. You are the other half of my soul. My *keeshla*. My fated mate and the female Deeka blessed me with. No matter what happens, I will always come for you."

Zara scoots up and kisses me. It starts out gently, but soon turns into a fiery passion that will never be extinguished. I roll again so she is beneath me once more and without words I show her my love for her until the sun rises and we both fall asleep in each other's arms.

CHAPTER 21

I quickly wash up and put on some clean clothes, my body aching in all the good ways after the most perfect night of my life. The village is teeming with activity as the sounds filter through the hide of my tent. Kyler and I slept half the morning away, as did a quarter of the village, I suspect. I know everyone has tended to sleep in the mornings after celebrations, usually nursing a headache from the wicked strong brew and heading to the healer's tent for some relief. It's why my mate is absent, although I'm about to go meet him.

Even though Kyler left not that long ago, I already miss him. God, I'm turning into a needy bitch. Except that I find I don't care. For the first time in my life, I'm not only in love, but that person loves me back. I plan on soaking up my man's affection every day for the rest of my life. I have a lot of missed love to make up for.

After running the brush through my hair, I leave my tent and head out to meet my mate. I'll miss this place a little when I'm gone. It's been my home for five months. It's where my best friends—sisters—and I lived together, even if it wasn't for very long. It's where I finally, for the first time in my life, started believing I was more than I'd been led to believe about myself. I feel like I've grown so much in not just this tent, but in this village. Surrounded by people who've shown me what family is truly about.

Tribespeople—both Tavikhi and human—nod or wave in greeting, and I smile and wave back. There's no sign of any Bohnari yet, but they probably all slept in their ship. I recall either Remi or London saying they stay a couple nights before heading back to Bohna. I'm glad Eloise will get another day with Johnna. It's crazy they landed on neighboring planets *and* both found a mate on that planet. Too bad they don't know what happened to their other two friends. Hopefully they made out as well as Eloise and Johnna did.

The healer's tent comes into view and my pace quickens. I step inside and my gaze zeroes in on Kyler who stands next to one of the raised platforms talking to Rojtar, who's sitting up and alert. A quick scan confirms he's the only wounded warrior that remains. The rest have all been cleared to leave for their own dwellings.

I'm so glad to see he's doing better. On our second night on this planet all those months ago when the Krijese—who at the time had been Tavikhi enemies—attacked the human settlement, Rojtar helped us escape. He's one of the youngest warriors—early-to-mid-twenties, I think—and one of the sweetest. I know how much he wants a mate, too, so I hope he finds one, one of these days.

As though sensing my eyes on him, Kyler turns and spots me. I give him a small wave. His mating marks darken and a flash of light shines from his pupils. An answering heat warms the inside of my chest, and I know it's the other half of his soul light. I'm still getting used to not only the sensation, but the fact that the phenomenon occurs in the first place. I mean, before it happened to me, I never would have believed that an alien race could literally share a part of their soul with another person.

"You should be able to return to your own tent tomorrow," Kyler tells Rojtar. "But you will need to wait a few more turns before it is safe to spar again. Even light training. You do not want to re-injure yourself."

I press my lips together to fight the smile that threatens at the disgruntled look Rojtar sends my mate. I'm sure it can't be easy for him to be laid up in bed recovering, but from what I understand, he nearly died. Kyler raises one of his brow bones until finally the young warrior nods. He claps Rojtar on the shoulder and joins me on the far side of the tent.

His tail wraps around my waist and he tugs me into his arms. We meet for a kiss, and I run my hands over his shoulders. He's hard against my belly and if we didn't have an audience I might take advantage of it, but sadly, I'll have to wait until we get back to his tent.

"Greetings, *keeshla*," Kyler says when we separate. "How are you feeling?"

The innocent question makes my cheeks heat because I'm not sure if he means in general or if he's asking if my pussy's recovered from the hammering he gave it all night long.

"I missed you." As much as it's torture for both of us, I can't help but rub myself against him.

His pupils dilate and he groans. "You are a cruel female."

"I'll make it up to you later. How's that?" I keep my voice lowered even though Rojtar is all the way on the other side of the vast space.

Kyler growls, and damn if it doesn't make me wet. "How will you make it up to me?"

My tongue flicks out and wets my lips. "Maybe I'll introduce you to a little thing called a blowjob. I've been wanting to know how good you taste."

His nostrils flare as though scenting my arousal. I squirm a little and squeeze my thighs together to try and ease the ache that's taken over. Damn it. I should have known better than to tease, because now all I'm going to be thinking about all day is sucking my man's cock.

"I will hold you to that bargain when we return to my tent this night, *keeshla*."

Hoo-whee, boy howdy. I actually can't wait. Kyler's made me feel so good, I want him to know the same pleasure he's given me. "It's a date, then."

I kiss him again. Only we're interrupted by the door flap swinging open and Zander and London walk inside. They come to a halt.

"Oh, sorry," London says. "We didn't mean to intrude."

"It is not an intrusion." Kyler takes a small step away but doesn't release the hold he has on me with his tail. He fists his chest. "Shefir. Shefira. How may I assist you?"

My friend and her mate exchange glances. She nods and Zander walks toward Rojtar, probably to check in on him. London's gaze shifts to me and a huge grin splits her lips. "I guess you're the lucky one who gets the news first…I'm pregnant."

"What?" I nearly screech and rush over to her, yanking myself out of Kyler's hold. "Are you fucking with me?"

She laughs. "No. We've been keeping it to ourselves, you know, just in case, but I'm starting to show and we figured it's safe now."

I glance down at her belly, which isn't noticeably different, and back up to her with a questioning look. "Can I?"

London nods and I slowly place my hands on her. Sure enough she has a bump. I stroke her and lean down to put my mouth close to her stomach.

"Hey little peanut, I'm your Auntie Zara." Tears well in my eyes and I get emotional, especially when, for a second, I think about Amelia and how she never got to have this. "I can't wait to meet you when you get here. You be nice to your mama in there though, all right. Don't kick too hard and watch out for her bladder."

I straighten and for one of the first times, I initiate a hug. I'm not sure if they'll ever come easily to me, but I'm going to keep practicing. Especially now that I'm going to be an aunt. "I'm so happy for you and Zander and I don't think I've ever said it, but…you're my sister and I love you."

London squeezes me hard. "I love you, too."

The embrace doesn't last long—I'm not there, yet—and we both wipe away our tears. I step back and lean against Kyler who lays his hands on my stomach and holds me close. I cover them with mine and wonder if he's thinking maybe one day I'll be the one having the baby.

"We just wanted to let Kyler know and see if there was any herb or medicine I should be taking," London says. "Thankfully, I haven't had any morning sickness since the first month, but this is the first Tavikhi-human to be born and we don't have any idea what to expect."

"Blessings on the impending birth of your kit," Kyler says above me. "There is the juice of the pellori plant that is beneficial for Tavikhi kits. I will get some for you and bring it to your tent later if that is acceptable?"

"You have our thanks." Zander returns and dips his head. I wonder if he's broken the news to Rojtar. "Come *keeshla*. We will make our announcement to the rest of our people during the evening meal and celebrate the approach of our first offspring before we bid farewell to our Bohnari brothers. The tribe will want to share in our happiness."

London waves goodbye to us and then she and Zander walk out of the healer's tent. I turn in Kyler's arms and stare up at him.

"I can't believe they're having a baby."

"With every new mating, the chances of a kit being born increases," he tells me. "It is a joyous thing for our people. For so long we have thought that we were going to see the end of the Tavikhi. But with this news, there is hope."

"What about you? Do you want children?" They're not really anything I've given thought to. Especially not with Clifton and Priscilla as their grandparents. God, that would have been a nightmare.

"I will admit I have always longed for kits, but I also know that Deeka decides who is blessed with them or not." Kyler grips my hips. "If we do not have any, it will not change how I feel about you. You are still my *keeshla*. The female who owns the other half of my soul light and I would not change that for anything. If we are lucky enough to have kits, then I will love them as fiercely as I love you."

Damn it. I sniff back tears because I've shed enough today. "I love you, too. I should have said it before last night, but I was scared. Not anymore though. I don't ever want you to wonder about or doubt my feelings for you. You are everything I never knew I wanted. Thank you for being patient. More important, thank you for loving me."

"You are an easy female to love." Kyler kisses me. "Let me say farewell to Rojtar and then we will join the tribe and celebrate our shefir and shefira's news with them."

I nod and wait while he speaks to the other warrior. He's not long and then he's back, locking his fingers with mine and guiding me outside. My gaze scans the village. Yes, we've seen loss, and there's still the potential threat of another Njeri attack, but that's a worry for another day. Tonight, I'm going to join my sisters and toast my friends and family.

When the party's over, I'm going to go back to the tent I plan on sharing with Kyler—my husband and mate—for the rest of my life, and I'll remind him how much I love him. Then, I'm going to rock his world.

EPILOGUE

Rojtar

Various aches linger in my body as I stride through the forest that runs alongside the human settlement with my sparring staff in hand and a sword slung from a belt around my waist. More than half a lunar cycle has passed since Kyler said I could return to hunting. A mellenje calls out and receives an echoing sound in return. Even the winged creatures are taunting me with their mating, reminding me that I am alone as always. I have no *keeshla* to laugh with or to share my furs with at night. Instead, I sleep in a large tent with other unmated warriors —most of whom are several seasons younger than me— and dream of the turn when Deeka provides me with a mate.

Except that turn may never come. Not when all the human females of age who belong to our tribe are already mated.

Life would be easier if one of the few unmated Tavikhi females was mine, but I have touched them all at their request and not a single one triggered my mating marks. I am not lucky like Zedam or our Bohnari brother and have my mate fall from the sky and crash land here.

My shefira has said that some unmated females remain at the human settlement. But in all the lunar cycles since the humans have been arriving on Tavikh, none have shown any interest in becoming part of our tribe. Not even after the Krijese who used to live under their King Armik's rule attacked and killed their people. I have been to the humans' gated village many times while escorting Sage back and forth during her apprenticeship with Kyler and not one female ever caught my eye. Zander and Zydon both said that a sinew cord tugged them toward their mates even before their marks were triggered by them. I have not experienced any tugs. Not once.

I scan my surroundings, staying alert for any signs of prey. Warm season is fully upon us, which means game should be plentiful soon. We made it through the cold season with our stores despite the increase in the number of tribespeople. After the attack that brought our shefira and her tribe sisters to the village, additional humans joined us as well. Mostly mated pairs with kits. We will need to spend the warm season replenishing all our supplies. Especially now that there are more kits on the way.

A shuffling sound draws my attention, and I freeze. My grip tightens on my weapon so I am prepared for whatever may come. More shuffling occurs, but with it comes voices. Human voices. I cannot tell who they are or how many are present. Despite the tentative trust that has been established between our two tribes, there are still humans who do not like the Tavikhi. Being careful not to make any noise or disturb any brush, I move forward keeping my steps light and soft.

"No, you have to do it this way." That sounds like a kit.

"This isn't my first snare, Carter. I know what I'm doing," a feminine voice replies with a hint of impatience.

Through the trees, I finally make out the two forms kneeling on the ground in front of a small burrow that probably housed a den of leburin at one time, but it is clear from the dirt around the opening that it is empty and has been for quite some time. Still, I watch and wait as they maneuver the string around. Or at least as the adult female moves it. The kit is a male and much smaller than her.

I study them and it is clear from their features they are related. They both have hair color similar to Jodah's mate, Sage, although the kit's is a brighter shade. Their nose structure matches and they have the same point beneath their lips. It is difficult to tell for sure from this distance, but they appear to have the same eye color as well. Is she the kit's Nene?

While her technique is fine, there are much better ways to set a trap. Although it does not matter which way either of them do it, they will have nothing to catch from an empty burrow. I should interrupt and let them know they are wasting their time, but I am curious about the couple. They are not familiar to me despite my frequent trips here to escort Sage back and forth between our village and the human settlement. Although I have not returned since the night the shefira and her tribe sisters escaped the Krijese attack many lunar cycles ago.

The female finishes setting up the snare and then she and the kit back away and hide behind a trendafili bush. A whispered exclamation of pain comes quickly as well as a sound to be quiet. The sharp leaves of the flowering bush do hurt a bit, which is why we all take great care to avoid them. It would not have been my choice for a hiding place.

As the sun slowly moves across the sky, the female and the kit remain where they are. Their eyes do not stray far from the burrow entrance as they wait for prey that will never come. The sun has passed its zenith when the female loosens a curse.

"You're not supposed to swear," the kit lightly scolds.

The female glares and rises from her crouched position at the same time a male steps into the clearing. He is tall—although not as tall as a Tavikhi—and has broad shoulders and meaty arms. His leg coverings hang below a belly that sticks out slightly and is held up by a piece of leather. The male is much bigger than the female who appears to come no higher than the middle of my chest.

"What are you two doing out here alone?" he asks, coming closer before stopping a short distance away from them. "I told you I'd come along."

"I didn't want to inconvenience you. You have more important things to do." The female places a hand on the kit's shoulder and guides him slightly behind her.

"Carter and I are doing just fine. I appreciate your offer though."

My gaze takes in the female and kit. Despite the even tone of her words, both are rigid—the female more so—and eye the male with a hint of distrust. I study him harder. There is something in his gaze I do not like. Especially in the way he looks at the female.

"It's not safe being outside the settlement walls," the male tells her. "You need someone to look after you, Abby. A protector."

Abby. I repeat the name in my head and enjoy the way it sounds.

"I've already told you Lewis, I'm more than capable of taking care of myself and don't need your protection," her voice is firm. "It's perfectly safe as well. Those creepy aliens stopped attacking months ago and you know the purple alien leader told Gary and Adam that most of them had been killed anyway."

This *Lewis* takes a step forward and another. "What about wild animals? You know there are any number of predators out here who are just looking for easy prey to snap up."

Abby and the kit—Carter—move backwards away from the male trying to put more distance between them, but he continues creeping closer. A scent carries on the breeze. It is bitter, unpleasant, and familiar. I have often smelled the same odor from a small creature right before it is overrun by a larger one. It is fear and it comes from the female and the kit.

I step out from behind the tree. "The female is correct. They do not need you as a protector because they already have me."

As one, Abby and Carter whirl to face me with a screech and she places herself directly in front of the kit. The male —Lewis—narrows his eyes.

"What the fuck are you doing sneaking around out here, alien?"

Ignoring him, I turn to the female and kit. "Is all well? Would you like me to escort you back to the settlement?"

"Hey, I asked you a question." Lewis stomps closer with his fists clenched. "What the fuck are you doing here?"

I do not take my eyes off Abby who has not relaxed her stance and still keeps herself between me and the kit.

"We're fine," she says. "Both of you guys can go home."

The male reaches her and Carter and grabs her upper arm. My vision goes dark.

"Let's get out of here." He tugs her harder than he should because she winces and tries to remove herself from his grip but he doesn't release her.

She makes a pained sound and flinches. Carter hits the males arm repeatedly.

"Let her go," he cries out.

My sword is out of my belt and at the male's throat before he can blink. "Take your hand off the female."

He does not move fast enough for me so I jab the tip into his neck to prick his skin and draw blood. Fear and hatred flash in his eyes and in less than a beat he releases Abby with a shove. She stumbles away, but steadies herself and drags the kit to her. She wraps her arms around him and holds him close. Her breathing is loud in my ears.

"Unless you want another taste of my blade, I would suggest you turn around and return to the human settlement." He will not get another warning. No one lays a hand on a female with intent to harm.

Lewis glares at me with pure hatred and then shifts his gaze to Abby and Carter before returning it to me. He walks slowly backward without taking his eyes off me. He jabs a finger in my direction and then in the female's. "You're going to regret this."

I do not move until he disappears from view and I can no longer scent him. Only then do I sheath my sword and turn toward Abby and Carter. I expect to be met with thanks and appreciation. Instead, fire spits from the female's gaze.

"Do you have any idea what you've just done?" she raises her voice and throws up her hands.

Confused at her anger, I blink. "I stopped that male from abusing you. His intentions were not good."

Abby scoffs. "No shit they weren't good, but now they're going to be worse. I had things handled, but then you had to come in and ruin everything."

I do not understand why she is upset. "That male grabbed you. Hurt you. He would have done worse if I had not intervened. No Tavikhi with honor would have let him do whatever he planned on doing."

She paces while the kit's gaze darts between her and me. The fear that had been present while the worthless male had his hand on her has slowly bled away. He remains quiet though while his—while Abby—mumbles as she walks back and forth. I catch a few words here and there, but I do not interrupt the conversation she has with herself. In time, she will understand why I could not just stand back.

Finally, she stops and faces the kit. "Carter, let's go."

He walks toward her with only a slight hesitation. His gaze continues shifting between us.

"Where are you going?"

"I'm going back to the settlement to apologize to Lewis and hope that's enough to cool his temper," Abby says as she takes Carter's hand and nearly drags him along behind her.

"Why would you apologize to that dishonorable male?" I follow them. "He is the one who wronged you."

She whirls on me. "Because if I don't, he's going to make my life complete hell. You get to go back to your village, while I have to live in the same place as that man and deal with the consequences of *your* actions. Lewis doesn't forget a slight."

"Then do not go back." I am not sure where the words come from, but once they are spoken, they make sense.

"Oh and just where do you expect us to go?"

"You can come with me to our village." The shefir has always stated that any humans who agree to contribute to the tribe are welcome. Abby and Carter should not be any different. I am not sure why I have made the offer, but there is something about this female that draws me to her. I do not want her to return to the human settlement.

She laughs but it is filled with bitterness. "Thanks, but no thanks. I'll take my chances with Lewis."

Once again, she turns her back to me and she and the kit set off toward their own village. He glances over his shoulder once. Abby not at all. I stand there a moment before following. I do not trust that other male and even if she does not want my protection, she will have it anyway. Deeka set her and the kit in my path for a reason. I will remain close by and watch out for Abby and Carter until that reason becomes clear.

Thank you so much for reading! Please consider leaving a review.

Want a bonus scene with Zara and Kyler? Sign up for my newsletter and receive not only the bonus, but you'll also get access to VIP content including early cover reveals, new release information, and you'll stay up-to-date on all things Warriors of Tavikh.

Get your bonus scene HERE

Have you read Fated to the Lost Warrior, the prequel to the Warriors of Tavikh series? Get your copy HERE.

For Abby and Rojtar's story, check out Fated to the Alien Protector

Warriors of Tavikh

Fated to the Alien Warrior
Fated to the Alien Hunter
Fated to the Alien Grump
Fated to the Alien Rebel
Fated to the Alien Healer
Fated to the Alien Protector

About the Author

Erin Hale resides in the South where the summer humidity sucks the breath right out of you. She's mom to the best dog on the planet. In her free time, she enjoys reading about swoon-worthy aliens (and secretly wishes one would land on Earth) and monsters alike. She also loves traveling the globe and can be seen most often in any of the pubs in the UK—where the weather is much more acceptable—with a raspberry gin and lemonade in hand.

To stay up-to-date on all her latest news, be sure to join her newsletter HERE!

I'd love for you to join my Discord reader group! It's where you'll get teasers and ALL the art I get commissioned (both SFW and NSFW). Find us in Erin Hale's Reader Group Discord

You can also join my Facebook reader group! You can find us in Erin Hale's Hideaway